ADVANCE PRAISE FOR *GREEN*

"Rae Spoon and Gem Hall craft a portrait of the many kinds of ghosts of trauma, colonization, and displacement—and the messy, persisting dollar pizza–eating queer and trans kids trying to get by and make something different, even if we don't know how."
—**LEAH LAKSHMI PIEPZNA-SAMARASINHA, author of** *Care Work* **and** *Dirty River*

"*Green Glass Ghosts* walks us through both the grit and camaraderie of underworld subcultures, with art and storytelling that doesn't alienate but encourages us to normalize our disarray."
—**CRISTY ROAD CARRERA, author of** *Next World Tarot* **and** *Spit and Passion*

"The collaboration between Gem Hall and Rae Spoon is tender, haunting, raw, and honest, asking of us to not only look back at our past selves but also to dream up different possibilities for our future. This is a book to hold in our hearts."
—**KAMA LA MACKEREL, author of** *ZOM-FAM*

"This book is wild and familiar, not unlike young queer lust, love, or existence. Reading this book is being lifted up, a firm reminder of still being here."
—**TARA-MICHELLE ZINIUK, editor of** *THIS Magazine* **and author of** *Whatever, Iceberg*; *Somewhere to Run From*; **and** *Emergency Contact*

"Lonely and spectral and hopeful. A tether for when you feel yourself floating away."
—**JAIME BURNET, musician and author of** *Crocuses Hatch from Snow*

"So sensitively and keenly observed, Rae Spoon's *Green Glass Ghosts* is a much-needed and timely work, beautifully and hauntingly illustrated by Gem Hall."
—**IMOGEN DI SAPIA, associate member of the European Roma Institute for Arts and Culture and creator of** *The Selkie: Weaving & the Wild Feminine*

GREEN GLASS GHOSTS

GREEN GLASS
GHOSTS

RAE SPOON
ILLUSTRATED BY GEM HALL

ARSENAL PULP PRESS
VANCOUVER

ARSENAL PULP PRESS
Suite 202 – 211 East Georgia St.
Vancouver, BC V6A 1Z6
Canada
arsenalpulp.com

The publisher gratefully acknowledges the support of the Canada Council for the Arts and the British Columbia Arts Council for its publishing program, and the Government of Canada, and the Government of British Columbia (through the Book Publishing Tax Credit Program), for its publishing activities.

Arsenal Pulp Press acknowledges the xʷməθkʷəy̓əm (Musqueam), Sḵwx̱wú7mesh (Squamish), and səl̓ilwətaʔɬ (Tsleil-Waututh) Nations, custodians of the traditional, ancestral, and unceded territories where our office is located. We pay respect to their histories, traditions, and continuous living cultures and commit to accountability, respectful relations, and friendship.

This is a work of fiction. Any resemblance of characters to persons either living or deceased is purely coincidental.

Permission to reprint lyrics from "Monster Truck Rally" provided courtesy of Angel Hall.

Cover illustrations by Gem Hall
Cover and text design by Jazmin Welch
Edited by Shirarose Wilensky
Copy edited by Linda Pruessen
Proofread by Alison Strobel

Printed and bound in Canada

Library and Archives Canada Cataloguing in Publication:
Title: Green glass ghosts / Rae Spoon ; illustrated by Gem Hall.
Names: Spoon, Rae, author. | Hall, Gem, 1986– illustrator.
Identifiers: Canadiana (print) 20200323245 | Canadiana (ebook) 2020032330X |
    ISBN 9781551528380 (softcover) | ISBN 9781551528397 (HTML)
Classification: LCC PS8637.P66 G74 2021 | DDC jC813/.6—dc23

For Vic Horvath

PROLOGUE

"Did you know," I said, "that Mary once threw me out of their house in the middle of the night for saying that Jewel's poetry sucks?"

Sam howled. "Yesterday, when I tried to bring up leaving the first time, Mary dropped my house keys into a full cup of coffee."

We laughed until there was a friendly pause. We were at the Denny's near Banff Trail Station in Calgary, where the servers had been letting me drink coffee and smoke since I was fourteen. A little over a year ago, some friends and I had celebrated the new millennium here by passing around a champagne bottle with a straw under the table at midnight. I'd met Sam through Mary, a mutual ex they'd come to visit for a couple of weeks. Mary was the type of person who was filled with love for everyone and really very kind, but a quarter of the time you had to tiptoe around them or they would explode on you. Earlier that day, Sam and I had escaped from

"You should come visit me in Vancouver. It would be so fun."

Mary's parents' house on a city bus with all of Sam's bags after they'd tried to push Sam down the stairs. All Sam did was tell Mary they had to fly home to Vancouver that night.

We leaned over our steaming coffee mugs and chatted conspiratorially, trading stories about other things Mary had done, our mood bolstered by the narrow escape. We shared the same flaw of returning many times to the people who have caused us harm.

Then Sam said, "You should come visit me in Vancouver. It would be so fun. You can fly youth standby. A hundred bucks and an hour later you'll be in Vancouver. You can stay with me at my parents' house."

I was silent for a while as I considered it. I'd just turned nineteen, and it felt like time was running out for me.

The café where I was working kept giving me fewer hours. I was barely able to pay my rent. Thank goodness for the tips I made and the odd show I played for extra money. I always showed up for my morning shifts at six, even if I was still a bit drunk. And I paid for all the beer I drank when I fell asleep on the couch that one time. I did get in trouble with the manager for yelling outside the café when it was closed a week or so ago. I guess they heard me from their apartment, which was right above.

Ugh, and then there was dating. On top of the on-again, off-again thing with the mutual ex, I was kind of seeing someone who'd bullied me in junior high. It turned out they were also queer, but things between us would often get really bad when we'd been out drinking. I hadn't seen them since they threw a cordless phone at me and screamed that I was fucked up and should get help. I couldn't remember what I'd said to them, so I told them to get out of my house and locked the door behind them. After I passed out, the sound of my window sliding open woke me up. They were sniffling and saying they loved me as they climbed in and fell to the floor. I played dead as they crawled into my bed and fell asleep with their arm around me. "I love you," they whispered before passing out. I pretended to be asleep in the morning when they left for work.

It turned out they were also queer, but things between us would often get really bad when we'd been out drinking.

Anyway, no real reason to stay for either of them.

"How will I find you in Vancouver?" I asked Sam.

"Take this bus," they said, scrawling with a pencil on their napkin. "It's the same name as the street it goes down."

"Granville?" I asked.

"Yeah, take it to Granville and Davie. If you don't make your flight, you can call my parents' house collect at this number." They scrawled that on the other side of the napkin. "Otherwise, I'll be standing there, waiting for you to get off the bus."

CHAPTER 1

Granville Street

Sitting on the bus, I peered at the words scrawled on the napkin I pulled out of my pocket. I scanned the letters closely, and then checked them against the words on the street signs as they whipped by at the intersections. They were the same. I felt brief relief, until it eroded beneath the terror of never having gone anywhere alone before. Every few minutes, I second-guessed myself, pulled out the napkin, and did the whole thing all over again.

I strained to look out the window around my guitar, which I had placed between my legs with the headstock sticking up in front of my face. It was late May, so when I'd left, Calgary was still all brown grass with dirt blowing around. Here, the grass was electric green and there were lush plants and flowers growing everywhere. The huge hedges in front of the giant houses along Granville Street were shorn to be all the same height. These houses were not like the overnight McMansions

in Calgary. They were made of brick and wood, and it looked like each sloped roof and turret had been placed deliberately.

After the repetitive jolting stops at intersections, a bridge appeared out of nowhere. The bus was suddenly high above the water, with a view on both sides. On the left was another bridge full of cars, and then the open Pacific Ocean full of tankers. On the right was the sparkling globe of the science centre that was built for Expo 86. I felt a pang remembering the pilgrimage we'd made to Vancouver when I was a kid to go to the World's Fair. At the last minute my father had decided the fair was part of an elaborate global plot. Instead of going, we stayed inside my great-aunt's house and waited to make the long drive home.

Now I felt like I could reach out and touch the glittering sphere. I turned my attention to the boats bobbing in the gaping blue on my left and smiled as the bus sped towards the city of green glass condo towers ahead of me.

Halfway over the bridge the bus speaker crackled, announcing Davie Street. I scrambled to get my backpack on and my guitar out in front of me. It was always a trick to make it out the doors in time with such awkward luggage.

I saw Sam before the bus doors opened. I never think people are going to show up when they say they will, but there Sam was, standing on the corner with another person.

I never think people are going to show up when they say they will.

"You made it!" Sam said, clapping me on the back. "This is Riki."

"Welcome to the Left Coast!" Riki said, with a debonair tip of an imaginary hat.

I blushed. Riki had shaggy, curly hair that almost covered their eyes.

"Let's go to the beach!" Sam said and started walking down Davie Street. "How was your flight?"

"It was great!" I said. It was only the third airplane I'd ever been on in my life, and a lot bigger than the one I took to Kelowna one summer. The best part this time was that it flew right over Kelowna.

As we walked down Davie, the rainbow flags started popping up. I had seen a small rainbow sticker or two pressed surreptitiously inside a bookstore or café door in Calgary, but this entire street was lined on both sides with big rainbow flags. I felt myself walking taller. We passed café patios with tables mostly full of men of all ages chatting to each other. Some held dogs on leashes, and others were holding hands right out in the open. I had done that sort of thing in high school, with grave consequences, but I'd never seen adults do it. I tried not to gape.

At the end of the street, we hit the beach. It was now around five o'clock, and the golden light shone straight into my eyes across the water.

"This is Sunset Beach," Sam said, stopping to squint out at the horizon. Riki kept walking towards the water like they hadn't noticed.

Sam turned and pointed behind us at a building just across the road from the beach. "That skyscraper was made by a famous architect. Vancouver City Hall hired them to design a building that represented the city. A lot of people were angry when they found out what the architect wanted to build."

I looked up and down the long circular column with the upside-down cone where the building hit the ground. There was a single tree growing out of the top of it. "What is it?" I asked.

"It's a needle," Sam said. "You know, because of all of the drugs here."

"Uh-huh," I said. Now I could see the needle injecting itself into the ground, with a tree for a plunger at the very top of the building. I didn't totally know what Sam meant about drugs, but there was a waft of weed—or maybe several wafts, coming from all over the beach.

I looked out at the tankers in the ocean. They were as big as some of the buildings on the shore, if those buildings had somehow fallen sideways. How were they were being held up by the water? I started to feel weightless and heavy at the same time, as if I were standing on nothing. The sun was even lower now, and I felt like I could see the shadows moving.

It's okay, I told myself. Over the last year I had learned how to not slip into a panic attack.

A hacky sack crossed my path and I looked up to see a barefoot, shirtless person wearing pants made out of patches of different fabric running towards me. I picked up the worn beanbag and tossed it to them. I had the urge to join their circle but sat down on a nearby log instead.

I spotted Riki making the rounds. They seemed to know everyone on the beach, and were busy chatting, slapping people's hands, and laughing.

Sam sat down beside me. "How are you doing?"

"It felt good to leave," I said. "But I feel like I'm spinning, being so far away."

"It's going to be way better for you here. I mean, the music scene is better, and there's way more people who are queer. I think you did the right thing."

"Yeah, there was nothing much for me there," I whispered, pushing away any thoughts of something or someone that I should miss.

The sun started to sink below the water as we walked away from the beach, past the early evening throng on Davie Street and then the blocks and blocks of old apartment buildings. Everything went from gold to grey. I grinned, looking at Riki and then at Sam, who was holding my backpack, so I was only in charge of carrying my guitar. After a while, the buildings changed to concrete and glass and stretched higher, the condos standing guard in lines.

"I hope my BMX is still here," Sam said. "Pete said they'd keep an eye on it."

I nodded solemnly, wondering who Pete was.

Sam made a sharp turn towards one of the identical towers. "Oh, good," they said, pointing to a small chrome bike covered in stickers that was locked to the otherwise empty rack out front.

They pulled out a small piece of plastic and put it up against the door. A little green light came on, and the door beeped and unlocked. I tried not to ask what it was as we all walked inside.

"Hey, Pete!" Sam called out to a person in a uniform sitting at a desk with a bunch of TV screens behind it. "Thanks for watching my bike!"

"No problem," Pete said, smiling.

We piled into the elevator and Sam pressed 6. After the door closed they said, "So before we get up there I'll warn

"My dad behaves better when there are guests around."

you, my house is kind of big. My dad bought half a floor of this condo building." Sam's expression was a combination of scared and ashamed. "It's good 'cause this way I don't see my dad on my side often. Now that my sister moved out, I fight with them a lot more. My mom lets me have friends stay in the extra rooms. My dad behaves better when there are guests around."

I nodded, bracing myself not to react to the apartment or show my apprehension about the unpredictable grizzly bear that was Sam's dad. But when we walked in the door my mouth fell open. The ceiling was higher than any I'd ever seen. I was pretty sure the TV in the living room was the largest one on Earth. There was marble everywhere: the floor, the kitchen, the fireplace.

As we shuffled down the hall, Sam whispered, "That's my father's office." They pointed into a room filled with books, a huge desk, a leather easy chair, and a giant TV. "When they're home they mostly hang out in there. They won't give you trouble, but it's good to not bother them. Just try to walk past without looking in."

Sam grabbed my arm. "Come on. I'll show you your room." We walked to the end of a long hallway. "This is my room, and this will be yours right next to it. You have your own bathroom in there, too. Go settle in, and Riki and I will come grab you in a bit."

I pushed the door almost closed behind me, unsure if I was allowed to close it fully. I flopped on the soft bed with my shoes still on and pictured my thin mattress that I'd dragged into the alley behind my basement apartment in the pre-dawn darkness. I wondered if anyone had found it before it got too dirty to use. I wasn't really talking to my mother much anymore since I'd came out to them over the phone with an abrupt "I drink. I smoke. I'm gay." So I couldn't exactly give them the mattress back.

I started to feel like I was spinning backwards. After a full revolution, I kicked my shoes off and got up to shake off my thoughts. I went into the bathroom and inspected the jets in the tub and the strange shower head the size of a dinner plate with holes all over it.

I sat on the toilet to piss and stayed there longer than I needed to, only returning to my body because I noticed my feet felt really warm. I reached down and touched the floor. After flushing the toilet, I lay down on the heated tiles. The warmth moved through my back and into my chest. My heartbeat

slowed down for the first time since I'd given my key to my roommate in Calgary that morning.

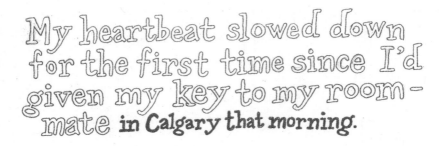

My heartbeat slowed down for the first time since I'd given my key to my room-mate in Calgary that morning.

I heard a knock on the bedroom door and called out, "Come in!"

"Are you in the bathroom?" Sam asked.

"Yeah, but I'm decent," I said.

They cracked open the bathroom door and stuck their head in. "Oh, I see you've found the heated floor. I do that all the time, too. It's the best when you're soaked from biking and you need to warm up. Riki and I are going to smoke on the big front balcony since my mom's not home from squash until nine. You want to join us?"

I usually smoked a pack of twenty-five a day. Somehow, I hadn't really thought a lot about smoking, but now the urge hit me hard, like a bad smell.

"Yeah," I said, fumbling around in the pocket of my sweat-shirt for my cigarettes as I stood up.

We all made the trek back down the impossibly long hallway. Passing the study again, I practised not looking in. I could see out of the corner of my eye that it was still dark. We kept walking until we hit the kitchen and living room. At the very end of the apartment was a sliding glass door. Sam opened it, and Riki and I slipped out after them.

The balcony was bigger than my whole apartment in Calgary. The smell of seaweed hit me as we leaned our elbows on the railing and lit our cigarettes. I slowly exhaled and took in the street below that ended at the dark harbour. Behind the opaque, almost black water loomed the blurred shadows of tree-covered mountains with a little white snow on top.

"My friends are having a party tonight. Do you want to go?" Riki said. "We could walk there in about twenty minutes, and they should be selling beer."

"Sure," I replied. I could use a beer. I'd been tempted to buy one on the plane, but I was too shy to ask.

CHAPTER 2

Downstairs in the condo lobby Pete's chair was empty. Sam patted the seat of their BMX as we walked past, and I heard the door lock automatically behind us as we went down the hill away from Davie Street and turned right at a sign that said *W Hastings St.*

The same condos seemed to be repeating themselves. Sam pointed out the only different one, saying, "That one's supposed to be earthquake proof." It looked almost like a box on a pedestal.

"Cool!" I said, and Riki nodded.

"Is yours?" I asked Sam.

"No. You'd think it would be for the money my dad paid for it. Everyone here says there's going to be a huge earthquake any day now. The Big One. But I haven't felt one do much more than shake the dishes, so who knows?"

Riki chimed in. "The earthquakes up here are nothing compared to the ones back home in California, but they do say that Vancouver is going to slide right into the ocean one day." They scuffed the ground with a small kick at a tiny rock, grinned, and then kept walking.

"Why wouldn't they make all the buildings earthquake proof if they know one is coming?" I asked.

Sam shrugged.

At the next red light we arrived at a street with a familiar name. We were crossing Granville again.

"The SkyTrain station's there. It'll get you all over town fast." Sam said, pointing up the hill.

"Like the CTrain?" I asked.

"Yeah, except it's up in the air some of the time, and it's way faster." Sam chuckled.

We passed a park on our right with a giant war memorial, and then everything around us was old, not like the neighbourhood with all the rainbow flags, but as if the buildings had been forgotten by whoever owned them. It was dark out, and I couldn't smell the ocean anymore. Another smell started to build up in my nose, one that reminded me of the outhouses when I went camping in the mountains in Kananaskis.

We crossed another street and I noticed there were no more people in suits with briefcases. I tripped on something and it skittered ahead of me on the ground. I bent down to pick it up and saw it was a piece of white tape with handwriting on both sides in different colours. *Repent Sinner*, it read.

Repent Sinner, it read.
Those words made my skin jump.

Those words made my skin jump. In high school I used to be overtaken by moments of believing the world was ending or Jesus was coming back for the Rapture. I'd only stopped going to church three years ago, after I moved to my grandma's house. And I had just kicked having all-out panic attacks about going to hell. I'd exorcized my fear by pretending I didn't care.

I dropped the tape and grunted, "Whatever."

"Those are all over the Downtown Eastside," Sam said. "Some people say this person who sits outside the old Woodward's Building preaching all day makes them, but no one really knows."

"What's that place?" I pointed to a sign that said *Blunt Brothers*. There were neon-green leaves in the window all around it.

"Oh, that place and the one next to it are cafés where you can smoke pot."

"Pretty cool," I said, wondering how they dealt with the police.

I looked up and saw a big red *W* on top of a boarded-up building.

"That's the Woodward's Building," Sam said. "The old department store closed a little while ago, and now the whole city is fighting over what to do with it. A lot of the people around here need housing, but rich people want to put more condos in it. I think it's going to be a long time before they figure it out." Sam stopped. "We're here."

Riki asked some people sitting in the doorway if they would mind moving. They did it in such a chill way that they seemed happy to oblige. Riki banged hard on the door. We waited, but no one opened it. The entryway smelled more like piss than downtown Calgary after the Stampede. I wasn't sure how long I could stand there, but it didn't seem to be bothering Riki or Sam at all. I tried holding my breath, and then I tried breathing through my mouth, and then I thought about the piss-air in my mouth and went back to using my nose.

"We're a bit early," Riki said. "Usually someone stays at the door during parties." They banged on the door a couple more times.

Finally, I heard footsteps pounding down the stairs and a muffled voice called, "Coming!"

The door swung open and a short bald person with a young face beckoned us in. "Riki!" they said, putting their arm around Riki's neck. "Come in, come in."

The piss smell stayed in my nose as I walked up the stairs, which were covered in old tile with cracks that showed the dust-filled glue underneath. I tried to hold my breath again, but Riki's friend was walking too slowly. When I took another breath I realized the stench had been replaced by the smell of fresh paint.

As we went in the first doorway at the top of the stairs, Riki said, "Jeff, you remember Sam. And this is my friend who just moved here."

"Nice to meet you," Jeff said. When they smiled I could see some gaps in their teeth on the sides at the back.

"You too," I said, wondering if I should have reached to shake their hand.

"Okay, over here," Jeff said, flopping back onto a couch, picking up a lit cigarette from an ashtray on the coffee table, and dragging hard on it. Exhaling, they said, "Make yourself at home."

We all followed suit, flopping on the couches and pulling out our own cigarettes. We sat there smoking in silence, and I noticed an old television that was just showing static, with no sound.

"Riki, this is my experiment I told you about last week," Jeff said, pointing at the TV. "Do you want to see it?"

"Make yourself at home."

"Sure." Riki blew a couple of smoke rings and put their feet up on the coffee table covered in ashtrays full of butts and roaches.

Jeff stood up with their cigarette in their mouth and pulled a beat-up old camcorder out from under the TV. They sat back down in front of the screen and turned on the camcorder with a little beep. For a second I saw their foot appear on the television. *This can't be it,* I thought. Then they pointed the camera at the screen. Moving shapes started to appear and fold in on themselves. Jeff leaned one way, and the shapes started to change. They leaned another way, and the shapes changed again.

"It's a visual feedback loop," Jeff said out of the corner of their mouth. "I think it's an image of eternity."

"Cool, man," Riki said.

Jeff kept talking. "I can't believe no one figured this out yet. It's so simple, but I think there's more meaning in it than I can understand. I've been doing this all day and I can't control the shapes. I never know how they'll change, and they keep surprising me. I think there may be some sort of key in it. Something to help me understand the meaning." Jeff looked back at us for a moment and then continued. "This is huge, so don't tell anyone about it yet. I can't let this get out of my hands too soon."

"We won't tell anyone. Right?" Riki gestured to us, and we all nodded.

I coughed a bit on my cigarette smoke. Jeff seemed nice, but I'd heard my father say similar things a few times, right before they would end up in the hospital. Riki seemed to really like Jeff, though, so they couldn't be too much like my dad.

"Can I show you around?" Jeff asked, putting the camcorder down and shutting it off.

We all nodded again.

"Okay, so this level is the bar. It's also our kitchen. There are some rooms back there where some of us have studios and beds. I live here, and so do a couple others. We put on some of our exhibits and performances on this level, but the big space is upstairs."

We followed Jeff back out to the stairs and went up. The top level was a huge open room with hardwood flooring from end to end. In the middle of the floor was a canvas, and there was that paint smell again—and a burning smell, too.

"This is what's left over from our performance last night. An artist named Claude fried up some meat cubes on a hot plate and ate them. Then they drank some paint and threw it all up on this blank canvas. They declared that all art is dead and lit the canvas on fire, except the fire went out of control and Claude had to pick up the canvas and run out into the street with it. There are always so many cops around here and they saw the fire from a few blocks over. The cops called the fire department and all of a sudden there were sirens and lights everywhere. They shut down the whole block. Then they threatened to have us evicted. I apologized to them, but Claude was more concerned about getting their canvas back inside. I thought it would be cool to leave it here for the party tonight."

I inspected the painted chunks of meat on the canvas with the big burn mark in the middle and thought about the art on the walls in the café where I used to work. Some of it I liked. Some of it I didn't. I wasn't sure if I liked this painting.

Jeff continued. "Tonight we're hosting a human branding, and I liked the idea of the pieces being in the same room together. You know ... Art is dead. Our bodies are only art ... Or something."

My eyebrows shot up, but then I thought it was probably better to mask my skepticism.

"All right, I better go get the bar ready and set up the DJ stuff." Jeff started shuffling towards the stairs, and then suddenly turned back. "Oh, wait! I almost forgot to show you the best part. Come with me!"

We all walked to a dead end behind one of the far walls at the end of the room, where a dirty, knotted rope hung down from above. Jeff pulled the rope and, with a thunderous sound of metal on metal, a ladder came crashing down. Jeff climbed to the top and pushed on a trap door in the ceiling. It groaned as it opened.

"Come on up!" Jeff beckoned. Over his shoulder, I could see some stars.

Riki and Sam were behind me, so I had to start climbing, trying not to think about the height on top of the roof, and then the return trip, backing down the ladder. Jeff reached out for my arm and helped pull me outside. Then came Riki and Sam.

"Now this is a view, eh?" Jeff said. "Sometimes I bring my sleeping bag and camp out up here."

"Wow." Sam whistled.

There was a long pause as we mutually admired the lights of Vancouver, with all the buildings and the mountains crouching behind them.

"Well, I better get back," Jeff said. "You okay to find your way?"

"Sure," Riki said.

"I'm going to go down with you now, Jeff. I forgot to hit the can on the way in," Sam said.

The two of them disappeared back down the ladder before I realized it meant I'd be alone with Riki. While I was wondering what I should say, Riki walked to the far edge of the roof and stood with their back to me. They were wearing really big shorts that were cut off between their knee and ankle, a forest green short-sleeved football jersey, and scuffed-up skate shoes. I could see the knot on their hemp necklace, slightly to the left at the back of their neck.

I walked up beside them, crossed my arms, and looked out at the buildings. The red *W* was much closer now, and I could study the metal structure it sat on top of. It looked like an oil rig, lit up all over by tiny light bulbs. Well, kind of—a lot of them were burned out.

I stood beside Riki without saying anything. Ever since I'd discovered that most of the things my parents taught me as I was growing up were wrong, I'd learned how to fit in by subtly mimicking people. I would follow their lead until I figured out how to behave in a particular group. Holding my breath and counting helped calm my nerves. I started to wonder which one of us was going to talk first and if we were having some sort of contest.

"Cigarette?" Riki asked, turning towards me with one between their fingers and ending the stand-off.

"Sure," I said.

They pulled a silver Zippo out of their front pocket and flicked it on by snapping their fingers on the flint. Damn, they were cool. I lit the end of my smoke, feeling a little dizzy.

I turned my head towards the sound of people screaming at each other in the alley on the other side of the building. It sounded like they were going to kill each other.

I felt butterflies in my stomach
and turned to face forward again.

"Don't worry about it," Riki said. "It happens a lot around here. If you're not a part of it, you should stay out of it." They looked into my eyes.

I felt butterflies in my stomach and turned to face forward again. "So there are a lot of drugs around here?" I asked.

People in Calgary always talked about how if you moved to Vancouver, you would just end up back at home. They said there were no jobs here and it was dangerous, but I didn't really know what they meant. The people I knew who used hard drugs like cocaine did so with friends in their own living rooms. I had heard stories of people using heroin and crack, but they were always at least one person removed from me.

"Yeah, there are people doing a lot of crack, meth, heroin, you name it," Riki said. "But it's their neighbourhood and community, and they have their own ways of doing things. I wish the government would just make drugs free and the cops would leave everyone alone."

The screaming had stopped, and somebody was laughing and calling out now.

"Anyway, I sleep here sometimes." Riki paused, and then said, with a twinkle in their eye, "You get used to it."

Before I could wonder if we were having a moment, Sam clambered back up the ladder. "People are showing up!" they said breathlessly. "Get down here."

CHAPTER 3

I didn't want Riki to see me fight it out with my fear of heights, so I told them I was going to check out the view a little longer. I waited ten minutes, surveying the full circle of illuminated cityscape around me. Then I called on every power I could think of and backed shakily down through the hole in the roof. I lowered myself a bit and kicked into the dark, but my foot met with nothing. I repeated the action what felt like countless times. Finally, the first rung of the ladder arrived like an epiphany, and the screams in my head converted into the songs of a choir. I slowly backed all the way down to the ground, one rung at a time. When I got to the bottom I could hear voices from the other end of the room. Heights started to feel a bit less scary compared to being around all those people. I waited a moment, and then shuffled towards the sound.

In the big room a group of people were circling the barf canvas and pointing at different parts. Someone had set up an old reclining chair, maybe from a dentist's office or barbershop, at the far end of the room. A person covered in tattoos was cleaning the whole thing with disposable wipes. There was a beat-up old halogen lamp lighting the scene.

Sam buzzed across the floor and grabbed my hand. They laughed and said, "Come with me," pulling me downstairs to the second floor. They whispered, "I'll be right back," and slipped away.

People sat on all the couches, watching Jeff point the camcorder at the TV screen. Jeff held court, glowing with his discovery.

My palms started to sweat. A person with long hair stood behind the kitchen counter, and there was a sign up that said *beer $3*. I bought one, cracked it, and moved into a corner so I could watch everyone. Then I spotted Riki. They were high-fiving a bunch of the people on the couches.

Sam made their way over to my corner from the bar. "Having fun?" They tipped the can to their mouth.

"Yeah." I did the same. "I went to parties in high school where a bunch of art students from the college showed up, but all they did was make fun of us and say weird things. Once, one of them asked me if I was dressed up as obnoxious for Halloween."

Sam almost spit out some beer.

"These people seem a lot nicer," I said.

"They are," Sam said. "I'm so happy to be back in Vancouver, and not stuck at that private school at Shawnigan Lake. My parents are pissed, but now I'm in this alternative high school here. I should even graduate less than a year late."

"It must have sucked to be trapped out there," I said sympathetically. "I'm glad you ran away and I got to meet you. Thanks for letting me stay at your house."

"No problem. You're going to love it here!"

More and more people started arriving. I'd never really seen people like them. There was no uniform look I could pin down except that they all seemed to wear whatever they wanted. I think most of them were artists. I heard the words "my practice" a bunch of times. I practised playing my guitar a lot, but I'd never called it that.

Riki had finished their rounds. "Do you want to see where I'm setting up my studio?" they asked us.

"Sure, just let me grab another beer," I said, crushing my can a bit in my hand and feeling more confident.

I put three loonies down on the counter and another one in the tip jar. Buying a drink without tipping was bad luck. Riki led us to a door on the same floor and flicked on an overhead light in a windowless room. There were canvases against the wall and cans of spray paint on the floor, with a clear garbage bag of empty cans in the corner.

"I'm working on a show," Riki said, pulling out some of the canvases for us to look at. They were different colours, but they all had magazine cut-outs stuck to them. "I'm not sure where I'm going to exhibit them, but Jeff let me have this space to work on them 'til I figure it out.

"They're cool ... I like your art practice," I said, wondering if I'd used the right words.

They smiled. "Thanks."

Sam piped up, "You know, Riki plays music, too!"

"Cool! We should jam sometime." I was back in familiar territory. Music was all I really had left from growing up that I could still appreciate.

"Yeah, I'd like that," Riki said. "Ew, do you smell that?"

A waft of something besides paint had started to overtake the room. It smelled like burned hair with a sickly tinge of cooking meat.

"The branding must have started," Sam said.

"Why are they branding people anyway?" I asked, feeling sheepish.

"It's like Jeff said. The person is letting the artist use their body as a living canvas. It's art," Riki explained.

I still didn't understand, but against the feeling in my gut, I followed both of them towards the awful smell.

There were about sixty people upstairs now. I'd learned to count groups of people rapidly when playing shows where I got paid per person. Most were gathered around the reclining chair, where the halogen lamp gave the scene an eerie alien-autopsy feel. Riki and Sam scooted in front to sit cross-legged on the floor, and I followed them.

The person who had been wiping the chair down earlier was now wearing a white paper mask and holding a soldering gun. "All is impermanence," they proclaimed, turning to the crowd. "Our bodies are just energy. We can do what we want with them."

Then they leaned down and pushed the gun onto the arm of the person in the chair, slowly tracing a line that had already been drawn on with pen. I heard the smallest crackle and my stomach turned.

I flashed back to junior high and a time when a kid brought in a jar with bull's testicles in it after being out at their uncle's ranch all weekend castrating and branding bulls. The scarlet liquid in the jar had made me queasy, and the branding was starting to give me the same feeling. I didn't want to be so close to that kind of pain. The smell was building, and so was the tension on the face of the person in the chair. I looked at my hands, and then started making guitar chord shapes on my leg. But I stopped because I thought it might look weird. I exhaled as quietly as I could and looked back up. The branding was going more slowly than I could handle. *How long does it take to burn the shit out of someone's arm?* I wondered, almost swearing out loud. I went to pull on my beer and realized it was empty. That was it. I had to leave, or I was going to scream.

"I gotta pee," I whispered to Sam.

I tripped a bit as I got up, but everyone was too focused on the soldering gun to notice. I started to feel dizzy and moved quickly down the stairs. I pulled the bathroom door closed and fumbled with the lock. Leaning against the sink, I tried to catch myself, but I kept hearing the crackling sound, and when I looked down into the toilet it was the dirtiest one I'd ever seen. I dropped my empty beer can on the ground and puked all over the seat.

"Shit!" I said in a liquid slur.

I was used to throwing up when I went out with my friends, but that was because I made myself do it so I could keep drinking. I would announce I'd thrown up when I got back to our table at the bar, and everyone would cheers and yell, "Drink, drink, drink!"

I wasn't even drunk right now.

I grabbed some paper towels, wet them, and wiped down the toilet seat. Most of the vomit blended in with whatever was already on it. I flushed, dried the seat off with some toilet paper, and sat down to piss.

My body was a bit closer to steady, but I could feel a panic attack coming on. I told myself that I wasn't trapped anymore. I had my new beginning. No more parents, school, or church. I could be anyone I wanted now. I should be happy, not feel like I was standing on a glass floor in a tall building. I embraced the idea and slowed my breathing down. I cracked the door and walked back out into the room with the couches.

Jeff was standing behind the bar. "You okay?"

I must have still been a little green. "Yeah, I'm just tired. I moved here today."

"From where?"

"Calgary."

"Rough town. I hitchhiked through there once during the Stampede and almost got my lights knocked out a few times," Jeff said. "Well, we better celebrate. Have a beer on me."

"Thanks," I said, grabbing it off of the counter. "Mind if I sit down?"

"Sure." They wiped some ash off the bar and onto the floor with a dirty washcloth.

I pulled an ashtray from the coffee table onto the arm of my chair and held my beer on my knee. I established a holding pattern, like I would on any other night at a bar. Smoke a couple cigarettes. Drink a beer. Repeat. The panic slowly sloshed back down my throat to wherever beer went in my body. I started to feel at home in the chair, like I'd always been there. People trickled downstairs after the branding and sat on the chairs around me. I talked to them with ease. I was charming and they liked me. I couldn't remember their names

The panic slowly sloshed back down my throat to wherever beer went in my body.

after they told me, but I began to feel like I could understand what people were talking about.

Eventually, I felt a new warmth on my left side and realized that Riki was leaning into me as they talked to someone behind me. I could feel their back through the perforated fabric of their football jersey. I tried not to move or breathe in case they weren't doing it on purpose.

Slowly, people started to leave. Sam seemed to have met someone, a cute smiley person with short hair. When the room was mostly empty Sam came up to me and talked low in my ear. "Hey, I know it's your first night in town, but do you mind if I keep hanging out with this person?"

My adrenalin spiked. I hated walking alone at night; I'd been chased too often in my mom's neighbourhood in Calgary by kids who knew I was queer. I flicked my cigarette to cover up my shaking hands.

"Sure," I said as steadily as I could.

"Riki can walk back with you. They were going to stay over anyway."

Lightning shot through my legs and bugs jittered in my stomach. My side was just cooling off from where Riki had been leaning against me before they went to the washroom.

"Yeah, sure," I said. "I hope you two have fun."

Riki came back and we both high-fived Jeff and headed down the stairs. Outside, we walked past people standing in circles, and someone on a BMX hooted at us before we jumped out of the way as they biked down the sidewalk. A couple of blocks later a person with a hooded sweatshirt pulled low over their forehead crossed the street at full speed when they saw us and asked, "Do you want to buy some down?"

"Nah, we're good, thanks." Riki kept walking in the direction of Sam's place.

"Thanks," I said.

"It's fine," Riki said. "They're just selling so they can buy their own. This place has its own economy. You know, a lot of people are scared of this street. Some of the artists feel like they're being very progressive for stepping foot on it, but I grew up in a neighbourhood like this in California. People just want to get what they need, and the cops are more dangerous than anyone else. You should never call the cops down here. They bully and beat up people worse than anyone who's ever lived here. It's safe if you get that everyone has their own trip they might be on. Stay out of the way and you're good."

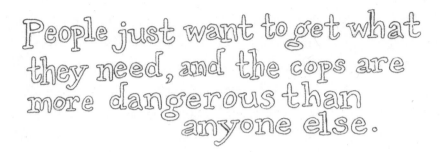

People just want to get what they need, and the cops are more dangerous than anyone else.

We walked in silence for a while. Retracing our steps was making me feel steadier.

"So you're from Calgary?" This was the first question Riki had asked me.

"Yeah, I grew up there," I replied. "You grew up in California?"

"Yeah, San Bernardino. Near LA. In the valley."

I'd never met anyone who grew up in the States. "Cool."

"My mom moved here a while ago, so I came up not long after. I met Sam at the alternative high school. I'm going to graduate soon."

"I was born in January, so I graduated when I was seventeen and had to wait six months before I could go to the bar, except for when I snuck in a couple times. People kept telling me to go to university if I wanted a job. I couldn't think of a job that I wanted besides music, so I just tried really hard to play shows. I did get some, but I couldn't see how to build from playing cafés to playing somewhere bigger like the Saddledome or something." I stopped myself, worried I may have sounded like I thought I was better at music than I was. I landed on ending with "And then I met Sam ..."

Riki didn't say anything back, so I bit my tongue. Sometimes I talked too much when I was nervous. I counted in my head so I would leave space for Riki to talk. I got up to forty-five before they said, "I had to go to California a couple months ago. A friend of mine died and a bunch of us had to go get their stuff. They were on a meditation retreat and fell off a cliff. I used to play music with them a lot, but I haven't really felt like it since I got back. Also, I broke up with my girlfriend when I got back and had to move in with my friend's mom. It was really hard to get my stuff back because my ex was so pissed off they barely let me into their parents' house where we were living."

I nodded, glad Riki was talking to me.

"You can't live with your mom?" I asked.

"Nah, they had me when they were fifteen. They stopped shooting up when we moved here, but things aren't good between us. Too much shit happened when I was growing up. I still talk to them, but it's always been more like I'm their parent. Plus, it would mess with both of our payments."

As we walked, the street slowly transformed back from old, forgotten buildings into the glass giants. I felt safe with Riki. They seemed tough, but like they would know when to run.

"Why don't the people on the street down at Jeff's hang out up here?" I asked.

"Well, whenever I see a line that no one's crossing I figure there's a wall there. Even if you can't see it. Someone's drawn a boundary and there must be a consequence for crossing it. People down by Jeff stay there because that's where they get the least shit from the cops. If they cross this line, they must be getting hurt for doing it."

"Did your mom get shit from the cops when you were growing up?"

"Yeah, but my mom came into that life from the outside, so we could escape from it a lot of the time. My grandma was a former model who drove a convertible. They used to swoop in and come get us, even if they were really pissed off. I got stranded a couple times hitchhiking when I was a kid, and they came to get me then, too. I really like surfing, so I would try to get to the beach from the valley. Most of the time I made it, but a couple times I needed their help to get home."

I nodded silently. Usually, I was the one with the big stories. This was the first time I'd ever met anyone with a life that seemed more surreal than mine.

After a couple more blocks I finally said, "I always wanted to run away in Calgary, but it was so cold, and even if I walked for an hour I'd barely be in the next neighbourhood. Sometimes I'd stand on one of the overpasses for a long time and think about jumping off, but I wasn't totally sure yet that there was no God, so I couldn't risk it. No one would let me stay with them, until my grandma ..." I saw Sam's building in front of us.

Pete buzzed us in and said, "Sam called and told me to give you the spare key."

"Thanks, Pete," Riki said.

"Sleep well," Pete said as the elevator doors closed.

"Did you know there's a squash court in this building?" Riki said.

"What? But Sam's mom goes somewhere else to play." I laughed.

"Yeah, it's probably even nicer. Sam's family is loaded."

"I gathered that." I chuckled. "Doesn't seem to make them get along any better, though."

"Nope, for sure not."

The elevator doors opened and Riki unlocked the condo door quietly. The door to Sam's father's study was closed, but I could see the blue light of the TV flashing at the bottom as we went past. We tiptoed to the end of the hall, where I was certain we would part ways. But Riki leaned over and whispered

53

in my ear, "Hey, can I sleep in your bed with you? I don't like sleeping alone in other people's places."

"Sure," I said.

We crept into my room and I turned on the light. I moved my backpack and guitar off the bed and pulled the covers back. I had slept in beds with lots of people and learned that the best thing to do was not be weird about it. It could mean many different things, and you always had to wait to find out which one it was.

I took off my shoes, pulled off my pants, and went into the bathroom in my boxer shorts and sock feet. I brushed my teeth and inspected my hair. I'd need to shave my head again soon. It was getting close to the tennis-ball look. When I came out Riki was already in bed, pressing the buttons on a little black box.

"Just shutting off my pager," they said. "You should get one. They're only five dollars a month and people can find you without having to call a phone. I've moved so many times, it really comes in handy."

"That would be awesome," I said, climbing under the blankets on the other side. "Do you need the light on to sleep?"

They shook their head and rolled over, turning their back to me.

I hit the switch. I used to have to sleep with a light, but in Vancouver with Riki I wasn't worried about the things that usually kept me awake. I yawned and snuggled into the bed on my side. My heart started racing, but I could also feel the emptiness of my stomach. All of the beer had been pissed out of my body, along with any notion of my own charm.

Riki rolled over to face my back. "Do you want to turn over so you can put your arm around me?"

"Yes," I replied.

I felt silly until Riki rolled the other way again, reminding me to do the same. They pulled my arm around their waist and smelled like sandalwood. I flattened my hand against their stomach and knew that I wouldn't have to worry about anything that night.

"Riki?"

"Yeah?"

"I'm glad I met you."

"Me too."

"I'm glad I met you."

"Me too."

CHAPTER 4

I woke up when I heard the door to my room slowly creak open.

"Hey you." There was a trace of amusement in Sam's voice. "You slept in. It's, like, noon."

I rolled over to face them. "Shit." Riki barely stirred. "Where did you go last night?"

"Do you want to come meet them?" Sam said, cocking their head.

"Sure." I stood up and pulled my pants over my boxers, running my hand over my hair.

I followed Sam into their room, past their messy bed, and onto their balcony. A person with a big smile was sitting in the chair farthest from the sliding door. "I'm Ocean," they said, extending a hand.

I reached over Sam to shake it. Sam and I lit cigarettes and puffed on them in silence, looking down at the grates on top of the building next to us. From this angle, the glass towers were especially thick. I couldn't make out the water anywhere, even though I knew it was all around us.

"Did you have fun last night?" Sam asked.

"Yeah. A different kind of party than back home. Usually people just drink until they're cross-eyed and break up fights," I said. "Jeff seems nice."

"They do some wild stuff there," Ocean chimed in. "I mean, the smell of that branding was too much for me."

"It did make me feel pretty sick," I admitted, making sure Riki wasn't within earshot.

"So, you and Riki." Sam smiled.

I felt my face turn bright red. "Yeah. They're really cool. Nothing happened last night, but we did cuddle." I looked over my shoulder again.

"It's nice to see Riki smile again."

I felt warm inside. In Calgary it was hard to find anyone to date. You had to be really sure someone was queer, because straight people would be super weird if you flirted with them by mistake. In Vancouver it seemed like you could find someone overnight—literally.

"Hey," Riki said, walking onto the balcony. "So, I need to make some money. Last night cleaned me out. You're a singer, right?"

"Yeah," I said.

"Do you want to go play downtown and see if we can make some cash for cigarettes?"

I didn't really need the cash yet, since I'd been saving my tips in Calgary for a while, but I wanted to go wherever Riki went. "Sure. I need some coffee, though."

"Let's make some here—and breakfast!" Sam piped up. "My mom just went shopping. We have eggs and waffles and veggie breakfast links."

"I should probably find somewhere to print some resumés," I said to Sam as we all walked back down the long hallway. "I need to get a job as soon as I can."

"You can use our printer," they shot back, already in the kitchen. "We have tons of paper. What phone number are you going to use? You can use my private line."

"Thanks. Do you have an answering machine?"

"Yeah. I'll change the message so your name is on it."

As quickly as four people could cook breakfast, the veggie sausages were sizzling in one pan, a whole bunch of eggs were frying in another, and the waffles were browning in Sam's giant toaster oven. Riki took a couple of breaks to smoke on the balcony and call back numbers that kept buzzing in on their pager. I tried not to stare at them through the glass sliding doors, but I couldn't help but look whenever they threw their head back in a big laugh. They seemed so happy, despite everything they'd told me last night. Maybe they could teach me how to show what I'd been through less.

"Want some syrup?" Sam said.

"Sure." I poured the syrup over my veggie sausages, wondering why it was so thin. "What kind is it?"

"Real maple syrup. Have you had it before?"

I shook my head. "Do you have any pancake syrup?"

"No. Mom won't let us have that kind of sugar in the house. This kind is more natural."

I was puzzled but took a bite of my sausage. "These aren't as bad as I thought they'd be," I said in spite of myself. "I mean, for not being meat, you know? They taste almost the same."

Sam chuckled, so I went on. "And the maple syrup tastes like a real tree!" I knew I'd gone too far and looked down at my plate.

"It is pretty tasty," Sam jumped in.

"Okay, I caught up on my messages," Riki said, sitting down at their plate and pouring syrup all over their food. They picked the waffles up with their fingers, setting them down again in between big bites. It made me feel better about how I was holding my fork like a pitchfork, unlike the others.

"We should busk on Granville," said Riki. "That's where the tourists are. You're supposed to have a permit, but we can just take off if the cops tell us to stop."

I thought about running away from trucks full of kids all through high school, carrying my guitar as I went. I was up for it. In Calgary I would hang out at this bar called the Mermaid with some guys who sang Bob Marley songs. I'd try to sing as loud as them. I used to be a quiet singer but learned to suck in a lot of wind to belt out "Stir It Up." All of Bob Marley's songs sounded good when we sang them as loud as possible.

This person named Brad who had their long blond hair in a single giant dreadlock would pour drinks and brag about the one time they went to Jamaica. "It's the best place in the world. You have to go. So spiritual," they'd say at least twice a night.

I asked them once if they'd ever been anywhere else, but they hadn't.

"I can play Bob Marley, Bob Dylan, and some Simon & Garfunkel," I told Riki. "Oh, and some of my own songs."

"That should do the trick." They smiled and downed the last of their waffles. "Do you want to come and get my drum with me? Maybe bring your guitar?"

"Sure."

At that moment, a person about my mother's age walked into the kitchen wearing a terry cloth headband and holding a squash racket. They were flushed and their smile looked real.

"Oh! I was wondering when you were going to get up," they said to the whole table in a singsong tone that made me believe they were happy to see us instead of pissed at us for sleeping in.

"Mom, this is my friend who's staying with us, and my friend Ocean."

"I'm Lynn. Welcome to Vancouver," they said, moving the racket to their left hand and shaking mine. "And hello, Ocean, nice to meet you. Riki, nice to see you! I'd better go shower. I had quite the match this morning."

With that they turned and walked down the hall, humming all the way, until they closed a door behind them.

"Your mom seems nice," I whispered to Sam.

"They are. They mostly keep my dad away from me since I ran away from home and came back. I don't know how such a good, kind person can be married to such a monster."

"My mom got a restraining order against my dad once," I said. "But then it expired and my dad kept showing up whenever they wanted. I had to chase them off the last time. My mom's dad sucked, too. They, like, ditched my grandma with six kids. My dad's dad shook me a lot and yelled at me when I was really little. I'm lucky they died when I was five. I don't know why dads suck so much sometimes."

I was relieved to be able to talk about it but surprised by the number of words that had flown out of my mouth.

"Well, my dad's really nice!" Ocean chimed in. "It's good to think more positively about people. If you expect people to be bad, they will be. Lots of men are really good."

I shrunk. That wasn't what I'd meant. There were plenty of men that I loved. But when I was growing up, everyone was always telling me to be nice no matter what. I didn't know how to be nice to a person who had hurt me so badly.

All at once, I felt like I was going to explode.

All at once, I felt like I was going to explode. My ears started to ring, but I knew I was the only one who could hear it. I grunted and stood up as slowly as I could so it wouldn't look like I was rushing. I had to get away before tears could fall. I put my plate in the sink and said, as steadily as I could, "Thanks for breakfast. I'm going to go have a shower."

I walked back to my room, but I never felt my feet touch the floor.

In the shower the smell of cigarette smoke came out of my hair when the water hit it. The stream stung my eyes as it rushed over my face, and a voice in my head kept mocking me for having said so much about my family. *Why can't you just learn to keep it in? You're so annoying. No one wants to hear about it.* I felt like I was getting close to wanting to hurt myself, and I was trying to stop it before it happened. *You need to be strong like Riki. They're so calm and they've been through so much more than you.* The thought of Riki started to draw me away from the chaos, so I tried to focus on them. I thought about how it felt to hold their stomach while they were breathing in their sleep.

I dried off with a soft towel and pulled on some big skater shorts that Sam had given me when they were visiting Calgary. The shorts were almost new and hung down to halfway between my calves and ankles. I pulled on some striped sports socks and an Expo 86 baseball shirt I'd bought at a garage sale. Lastly, I snapped my wallet chain around the front belt loop of my shorts and put my wallet in my back pocket.

When I came out of the bathroom, Riki was sitting on my bed. I looked in their direction but not into their eyes so I wouldn't blush.

"Ready?" Riki asked.

"Yeah," I said, resisting the urge to touch my face to see if it was still hot from crying. I pulled my guitar in its soft case onto my back, and we headed out.

When we got outside, Riki asked, "Do you have any change? We can get a bus over the bridge. It'll be way faster than walking."

"Sure," I said, fishing around for a couple of toonies and handing one over.

We walked down Pender Street, back towards where we'd gone to the party the night before. Riki turned on Granville, where we stood at a busy bus stop.

"Sometimes I stay in False Creek with my friend Meeka's mom, Kim. They have a spare room and I keep a bunch of my canvases in it," Riki said. "Kim's a brilliant playwright. Sometimes their girlfriend stays with them, too. Andy's also bipolar and recovering from heroin addiction, so they're on assistance, like me. Kim lives in co-op housing, so the rent is cheap."

I nodded but held in the fact that my father was also bipolar and schizophrenic. I was practising acting tough now.

A bus pulled up and we jumped on. It sped through downtown and hit Davie Street, and we got off the bus on the other side of the bridge.

"What's that smell?" I asked, waving my hand in front of my face.

"It's yeast. That's the Molson Brewery," Riki said, pointing at a big clock with a Molson logo.

I sneezed sharply.

"Allergies?" Riki asked.

I didn't answer except with a shrug.

Riki pulled out the big key ring that was clipped to their back belt loop and opened the front door of the building where they were staying. Inside, the lobby was covered in dark brown wood panelling and the carpet was light green. We took the elevator to the second floor, where the hallway smelled like all kinds of cooking. I could hear a TV as soon as Riki opened the door to one of the apartments.

"Kim, it's me!" Riki called out.

"Oh, hi!" A person with vivid red hair and wearing a silk patterned dressing gown came through the kitchen towards us as we were taking off our shoes.

"I came to get my drum," Riki said, giving Kim a hug.

"You can come here anytime! Oh, hello," they said warmly, hugging me as well.

"Nice to meet you," I said as a floral scent wafted from their dressing gown.

"Come in and have a cup of tea. Come meet Andy. What kind of tea do you like?"

Kim gripped one of my hands and pulled me into the living room, where another person was sitting on the couch. Andy reached out to shake my hand, and theirs was small in mine, which I wasn't used to. I tried not to stare at the scars on their arms and focus on their face instead.

"Hi," Andy said. "Sit down anywhere you want!"

Riki had disappeared, but I could hear them rummaging around somewhere. "What are you watching?" I asked, sitting down on the couch.

"It's called *Survivor*," Kim answered. "They put all of these people on an island with almost nothing and they have to work together. There are challenges for prizes like food. But they have to vote one of them off each week. The last person left at the end gets a million dollars."

"Oh, it's that new show." I scanned the beach scene and the people building shelters out of things they found lying around. "They eat bugs on it sometimes?"

"Yep," Andy said, grinning. I noticed they had more spaces than teeth in their mouth. They smiled widely, with no trace of self-consciousness, and I instantly liked them for that.

Riki came out of the back room with a huge drum slung over their back by a strap. "We should go while the tourists are still out."

"Oops, I forgot to make tea!" Kim cried. "Sorry. I haven't slept much the past few days. Don't worry, Riki. If it lasts a week I'll call my doctor."

Riki nodded and touched Kim's shoulder tenderly.

"That's okay," I said. It had been nice to sit and watch TV with them, even just for a minute.

When we were back out on the street Riki said, "We better walk over the bridge so we don't have to buy another bus ticket."

The walk across the bridge was windy and long. At one point we stopped and hung our heads over the side so that Riki could show me Granville Island below. There were so many people and cars going up and down the small streets, and tons of seagulls looking for food.

As we started walking again, Riki explained our strategy for busking. "Have you ever busked before?" they asked.

"Yeah. Once in Kelowna by the lake when I was a teen-ager. And I tried once in Calgary in front of a record store in Kensington, but the cars were louder than me. I gave up both times because no one gave me any money."

"The trick is to go in front of an empty building or a business you're sure won't make you move right away," Riki said. "There are way too many transit cops by the SkyTrain station, so we should stay closer to this end of Granville. It's a good street because a lot of people walk up and down it all the time."

"How about here?" I said, pointing to a boarded-up enclave that looked like it used to be the entrance to a movie theatre.

"Yeah, this should work. Can we use your guitar case for the money?"

I pulled out my guitar and spread the case open in front of us. It looked a bit slumped because it was only canvas and foam, but it would do the trick.

Riki reached into their pocket, pulled out a bunch of change, and threw it in. "We have to get things started somehow," they said.

I remembered Riki had said they had no money earlier, but I brushed the thought away.

Riki grinned and found a spot to sit beside me, throwing one leg up over the drum so that it was lying sideways. They rubbed the skin on their drum and turned to me. "Play a song, any song," they said.

Suddenly, I had stage fright in front of my audience of one. I delayed for a minute by tuning my guitar, and then decided to go with one of my songs, since I knew them the best. As I started the intro, Riki hit the drum quietly while staring intently at my hands. I sped up my playing a little and started to sing.

I sang every song I could think of, and Riki drummed along. I sang songs I had written, and also some Bob Dylan, Joni Mitchell, and Radiohead. Some people passing by seemed to like it, and some of them threw quarters. But many moved to walk farther away on the sidewalk, like we had some communicable disease, while others pretended they couldn't see us by looking anywhere else. Somehow this made me feel like they were staring right at me.

After more than an hour we had a fair amount of change in the case. When my fingers started to get tired I stopped and rubbed my hands together.

Riki put down their drum, leaned into my guitar case, and started scooping all the money into their pockets. "I'm going to go buy us some cigarettes and booze with this if that's cool," they said, not waiting for an answer. "Do you want to meet me later to go to a gay bar?"

"Sure."

"I'll walk you back to Sam's, and then I can come pick you up in a bit."

Sam's condo was dark, but when I squinted I could see that some of the furniture in the living room had been knocked over, ornaments and all. It felt like a crime scene on a TV show.

"Sam?" I called out in spite of my fear.

What if their father was home? I walked down the hallway, making no noise. I had learned how to place my feet silently when my own father was home.

Sam's bedroom door was ajar and the light was on. Their room wasn't trashed like the living room.

"Sam?" I whispered it this time.

"Out here," they answered from the balcony. Their voice sounded smaller than usual.

I rushed out like it was an emergency, but I could see when I got there that I was too late. Sam was curled up on a chair, holding one of their arms against their body with the other. Their face was red from crying.

"Oh, Sam—" I started.

"I'm okay," they interrupted. "My dad just got pissed off at me for putting the dishes into the dishwasher wrong and things got out of hand."

"It's not okay that your dad hurts you," I whispered, tears welling up in my eyes. I was trying not to fall down my own well of memories. My body hadn't forgotten, but I didn't want to make everything about me. I grappled my attention back to Sam. "Riki should be here any minute. They were thinking we could all go out?"

Sam brightened. "Where?"

"To a gay bar."

"Which one?"

There's more than one? I thought.

"It's not okay that your dad hurts you."

71

Then the cordless phone in Sam's hand rang, and they buzzed Riki in. "Can you help me to the washroom?" Sam whispered.

I nodded and helped them up, careful to not touch the half of their body they were favouring. By the time Riki got upstairs, I had assumed my regular position on the balcony, next to Sam's empty spot.

"I got you a present," Riki called from halfway down the hall. They joined me on the balcony and passed me an open pack of cigarettes.

"Thanks!" I said and slid one out.

"So, do you want to go out to the Village?"

"Hey," Sam said. They sat down without saying anything more. I knew Sam wasn't trying to hide anything from Riki. They just wanted the pain to be over.

Riki was on a different wavelength, looking eagerly back and forth between us. I wondered if Riki had noticed that the apartment was messed up on their way in, or that Sam was nursing their arm, but their excitement was infectious. Suddenly, the low place I'd fallen into when I found out Sam was hurt felt like somewhere I should pull us both out of, if I could.

CHAPTER 5

It felt like I'd already been in Vancouver for weeks, not barely twenty-four hours. The three of us were making jokes the whole short walk to the Village. Sam was quiet at first but slowly returned to their usual jovial self. I knew Sam was back when they showed us how they could do the grapevine faster than Riki and I could walk. They were crossing their feet over each other and giggling, until they misjudged a corner and fell into a hedge, sending us into screams of laughter. I tried to pull Sam out of the hedge with one hand, but Sam was laughing so hard their knees buckled and they fell back in again.

Davie Street, when we finally got there, looked different with the street lights on, and there were neon rainbow signs in a lot of the bar windows.

Riki suddenly stopped and said, "Wait, wait. I have more presents. I can't face the gays with only two beers under my belt." From a pocket, they produced a mickey of whiskey. "Let's drink before we get there. Way cheaper!"

After we finished half the mickey, Riki put the bottle under their belt at the front of their pants. "In case they check our pockets at the bar," they explained. "It's not a bathhouse night, so they won't be checking here—" They grabbed the front of their jeans.

I blushed and we all laughed.

We joined the line forming in front of a lighted sandstone building with a sign that said *Celebrities*. Riki reassured us again in a low whisper that it wasn't a "boys' night," so none of us would be turned away or humiliated for not being "the right kind of person." The throbbing bass spilled into the street whenever someone opened the doors. The bouncer peered closely at my Alberta learner's permit under a black light. I looked young for my age. Sometimes I had a hard time getting into movies rated fourteen and up.

"No body searches," Riki said when we got inside, grinning like a lion. "Let's go! Stick together."

We all grabbed each other's hands, with me in the middle, as Riki led the way through the crowd to the bar.

"You want a drink?" Riki asked me.

"Yeah, can I get you one?"

"Rum and Coke!" they yelled into my ear.

I could feel Riki lean into me for a moment and my chest started to soar. Sam had let go of my hand and was joking with one of the bartenders. I ordered the drinks and turned my attention to two people dancing in briefs on either side of the DJ booth. I wondered if it was their job or a hobby.

"Do you want to go smoke on the patio?" Riki asked. "You can't smoke inside anymore. It sucks."

I could feel a bunch of people pushing against me to get to the bar, so I grabbed the drinks and slid a ten towards the bartender, feeling like it was a pretty good tip. I handed a drink to Riki with a bow and made a smoking gesture to Sam. The three of us made a train through the crowd and ended up on a smoke-filled patio at the very back of the bar where it was a little quieter.

Riki knew a couple of the people there, and they joined our circle. I tried to remember their names as we were introduced and couldn't. I told myself it didn't matter. I leaned back against a railing like a cowboy and puffed away at my cigarette, leaving it in my mouth and nodding in agreement. Every time I put a new smoke in my mouth, Riki would make a big production out of lighting it for me. I looked around at everyone and felt weightless as the pressure of always measuring how I behaved lifted a bit. I glanced at Sam; they were smiling and moving freely, as if nothing had happened. The alcohol must have taken the edge off their pain. I felt tough, like we were all invincible.

Then I felt some hot breath in my ear. "I bet you think you're so butch." A muscular older person in a leather vest was leaning over the railing to hiss into my ear. "You're pretty strong, too, I bet," they said and grabbed my upper arm.

Lightning quick, I thought it was good they had chosen my arm instead of Sam's injured one. Then fear and rage were the only things I could feel.

"No, I actually don't care how strong I am," I replied, looking around for help. Riki and Sam were deep in conversation.

"Well, if you think you're so tough, you're going to have to prove it," they challenged.

I knew where this was going, although it usually came from straight people. I also knew there was no stopping it with talk. I dropped my half-smoked cigarette and stepped on it. The person leaning over me had written the script, and they weren't going to let anyone else change it. Using the element of surprise, I jolted myself free from their grip by dropping down to the ground like I was going to do the worm. Their angry hand was no match for my dead weight. Growing up, I'd had plenty of opportunities to learn the power of letting all my muscles go limp, usually when my father tried to carry me to the van to go see a Christian therapist or something.

But I couldn't rely on being lower than the crowd for safety. Kicking someone when they're down is in the skill set of any bully. Shock was my next defence. I screamed shrilly in my highest falsetto, "I'm not butch. I'm more of a princess. And like all princesses, I've got to dance the night away!"

Then I used speed, my final escape tactic: I leapt to my feet and ran into the bar before anyone could pursue me. I chose the DJ booth at the front of the room as my true north and waded as deep into the dancers on the floor as I could. I wasn't dancing—I was really there for cover—but I did have to move with the palpitating crowd. Somehow, I knew that if I stood still I would be in the way. Thankfully, I was shorter than most people. When I could sense that my adversary had not found me and probably wasn't going to, I noticed the dance floor dress code. It was hot, and I had the urge to pull off my shirt and tuck it into my back pocket too, but I knew that might get me kicked out. It was legal to take your shirt off, but no one like me was doing it unless they'd had surgery. I kept my shirt on and surrendered, at least for the time being.

Immersed in the dance floor, I couldn't fathom its end.

Immersed in the dance floor, I couldn't fathom its end. At times the music's throbbing beat would pause until it felt like it would never come back. Then spacey sounds would swell, somehow far off in the distance, and at the perfect moment—pow! The bass drum would kick in and everyone would go, "Whoop, whoop!" When the beat finally dropped everyone would jump up and down, ecstatically moving their bodies in unison.

The music soaked through me. I wasn't allowed to dance as a kid because of the whole Pentecostal thing, but for a minute I felt like I almost could. My body was electric, and when a hand touched my shoulder, turning me around, I didn't jump. It was Riki, a half-smirk on their face. My mind stopped on one thought: I wanted Riki. If I could be closer to them, I would be further from everything else. Whatever I had been before, whatever had happened to me, none of it would matter anymore.

I moved closer to Riki, making eye contact. They moved closer to me. Pressed up against them, I could feel the bottle they had hidden in their pants and wondered how it stayed there, impossibly suspended. Riki put their hand behind my head, holding on to my hair, holding eye contact, and pulled my head even closer. I moved in and put my mouth on theirs. It tasted like whiskey and heat. We stood still, kissing deeply.

Sam danced over to us, grinning, with Ocean, who must have just arrived, trailing behind. I reminded myself that everyone says hurtful things sometimes and decided to give Ocean another chance. We all started mimicking each other's movements, making up more and more absurd ones for the others to copy. We got in a line and pretended to be canoeing. Sam turned around and yelled something from the front of the canoe. "Portage!" Riki said from their spot in front of me, their mouth against my ear and their arm pointing up. We lifted our imaginary canoe together and followed Sam right off the dance floor. We carried it proudly past the bar, down the stairs, and out the front door. Outside, the canoe disappeared and our line dissolved into out-of-control laughter.

Sam chortled. "Did you see their faces?"

"I ran away to the dance floor because someone was trying to fight me on the patio," I told the group.

"Shit," Riki said. "Sorry we didn't see that."

"That's okay," I replied. "I've had a lot of people chase me because I look queer, but I've never had someone want to fight me because I supposedly think I'm tough. I mean, look at me."

They all nodded at my obvious lack of muscle.

"Ocean and I are going back to my place," Sam said. "Do you want to come with us?"

I gave Riki a look that said *I'm going where you're going*. So Riki said, "I want to walk around for a bit. You want to come with me?"

I nodded.

We hugged Sam and Ocean goodbye and watched them walk away holding hands down Davie Street until they crossed the road towards Coal Harbour and disappeared from view.

"I worry about Sam," I said. "Their dad really hurt them today."

Sam must have told Riki what happened because they said, "Me too. Their dad is gone now for a business trip, so they'll both be okay tonight."

"I slept with a knife under my pillow for years after my dad got kicked out of our house for good. I always thought there was a chance they would find their way back in. Sometimes I still wake up and feel like they're in the room with me."

"That sucks. They were pretty mean?" Riki asked.

"Yeah. In every way, I guess. I mean, I thought they just hit me and hurt me with their words, but when they moved out I remembered some of the other stuff they did. Really sick stuff. It's not so clear, but my body knows what happened. It feels like being boiled in poison to try to remember. Know what I mean?"

Those memories are back in Calgary now, I whispered in my mind.

"Yeah. My mom was too sick to protect me when I was a kid. A lot of fucked-up shit happened to me. I'm just glad I live in Vancouver now. Those memories are back in California."

I nodded and lit a cigarette. I was shaking a bit, thinking about my father, but I reminded myself that they would never find me here. *Those memories are back in Calgary now*, I whispered in my mind.

"Anyway," Riki said, changing the subject, "do you want to see something cool?"

I wanted whatever Riki wanted. I nodded.

"Come this way," they said.

They broke into a speed-walk, and I did the same. Then they broke into a run. I still had a lit cigarette in my hand, but I managed to keep up. We ran towards a dark patch with no lights. I could smell Riki as I trailed behind—the same sandalwood scent I'd noticed the night before, with a hint of cigarettes and sweat.

We were at the edge of the sand before I was able to see where the water started. The tide was high and there was only a thin strip of beach.

"Are you ready to see something magical?" Riki said.

"Yeah!"

Riki peered at the ground in the dark and found a piece of driftwood. They walked right to the water's edge, and a wave almost washed over their toes. They wound up and tossed the stick a couple metres out. A bright green light erupted all around the spot where it fell and speckled the water wherever the spray landed. My heart felt close to exploding with wonder.

"It's called phosphorescence," Riki said.

"What is it?" I hunted down a stick of my own and threw it as hard as I could, satisfied with the large glow it produced.

"It's from algae in the water. When you knock them together, they glow with the energy you created. They generate light."

"It's the same colour as the northern lights in Calgary. They move the same as this sometimes. Like liquid."

"Cool. I've never seen the northern lights." Riki pulled the bottle of whiskey out of their pants and sat down on a log. I sat down next to them.

"If it was any windier, the whole beach would have sparkles at the water's edge," Riki said. "I've seen it before. We could even go swimming. I'd like to have light all over my body."

Riki opened the bottle, took a swig, and held it out to me. The whiskey was warm from their body heat and burned on the way down. I thought I felt Riki's leg move closer to mine. Ever since the dance floor, I had been wondering if we would touch again. I dropped my hand onto my knee and saw their hand lying on their knee, pretty close to mine. I looked back out at the ocean, where the water was dark again. I decided to take a chance, but not a big one. Slowly, I moved my hand over and rested one of my fingers on Riki's thumb. They didn't move away, but they didn't move at all. I started to feel like I was plummeting towards the earth's core, but then Riki grabbed my finger in their palm, curling their hand around it like they were playing some sort of pull-my-finger joke. I decided not to mention that. Then Riki pulled my hand right into theirs, interlacing our fingers. A liquid light shot from my toes right up to my head and back again, like a waterfall was cascading from each end of my body and racing towards the other.

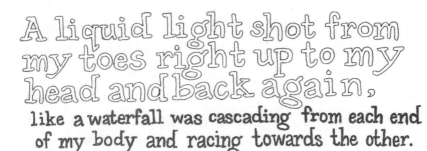

A liquid light shot from my toes right up to my head and back again, like a waterfall was cascading from each end of my body and racing towards the other.

We sat there like that for a while, until Riki said, "Do you want a cigarette?"

"Yeah."

Neither of us must have wanted to let go of the other's hand, so Riki put two cigarettes in their mouth, lit them, and then passed me one with their free hand.

"Do you want to stay with me tonight?" Riki asked.

"Sure. Do you think Sam'll worry?"

"Nah. They're busy right now. We can call in the morning to let Sam know we're okay."

"Okay."

"We can walk back over the bridge if you want. There might be buses still, but it's not that far from here. If it's not too cold out for you?"

I chuckled, remembering trying to pull a squeegee out of a frozen bucket to wash a car window at the gas station where I worked after high school.

"I'm okay," I said. "One last thing!"

I let go of Riki's hand and picked up a huge piece of driftwood. I tried not to look like I was struggling, but it was ten times as heavy as I thought it would be, since it was soaked through. With the branch braced against my stomach, I shuffled as close to the water's edge as I could. Then I heaved the wood into the ocean, and green light burst everywhere.

CHAPTER 6

I woke up sneezing on a mattress on the floor. The air smelled like yeast, and a train was going by outside, its horn blaring. I felt the sheets and blankets against my bare legs and stomach and realized I was naked. Well, I did have my socks on. I could see Riki's bare arm hanging out the other side of the bed. I smiled to myself. Now that I knew Riki liked me, it felt like I had figured out where I was supposed to be.

Riki's hand drum was lying on its side on a pile of crumpled-up clothes. There were a couple of empty cigarette packs and old coffee mugs on the small wooden box serving as a night-stand. I had only been in Vancouver for two nights now, I realized.

Riki stirred next to me. I must have been fidgeting and woken them up. "Hey," they said, rolling over and putting their arm around me.

"Morning," I said. "Hey, I think I need to get a job some-time soon, but I don't have a phone. Can you show me where you got that pager?"

"Sure. It's downtown. Really easy. You want coffee?"

"Yeah."

Riki stood up with their back to me, wearing only a pair of boxer shorts, and stretched as they looked out the window. They pulled a T-shirt out from under the drum and put it on, and then they picked up some rumpled shorts from the day before that still had their key ring and wallet hanging from them and pulled them up over their hips.

"Come out when you're ready," Riki said with a wink and left the room.

I scanned the room for my own clothes and found them under the empty bottle we'd polished off after we rolled around naked for a while. I stood it up on the wooden box next to the bed and sat up on the mattress that was barely higher than the floor, stubbornly pulling my clothes on with-out standing up. I lay there for a moment, clothed and staring at the ceiling. Then I stood up too quickly and had to hold on to the wall for a minute. After I recovered my balance, I tried to push my hair down flat and walked out.

"Good morning, sunshine!" Kim said as I came into the kitchen rubbing my eyes.

"Good morning!" I said, my voice breaking as I tried, and failed, to match Kim's cheery tone.

Kim and Riki both chuckled. Riki was leaning over the stove, pouring coffee out of a stovetop pot into two mugs. "It's espresso," they said. "Do you want to add some water?"

"Yeah, that'd be great."

Riki grabbed the kettle on the burner next to the coffee pot and sloshed some hot water into both mugs. "We can sit out on the balcony," they said.

Outside, the morning had started without us. Kim's housing co-op backed onto a long neon-green lawn with cement paths running through it. Riki and I settled into two mismatched plastic chairs and watched the people coming and going.

"I call it the spandex superhighway," Riki said, gesturing towards a group of runners in bright exercise gear.

Riki was right. As soon as that group disappeared another one showed up, and then a lone jogger, and then a couple. It never ended.

"I don't like running," I said. "It reminds me of being chased."

Riki nodded thoughtfully. "Yeah. I wonder what's chasing all of them?"

"Probably just death," I said.

Riki laughed. "Well, death is never that easy to predict. It might be waiting in the direction they're running."

I blew on my coffee and slurped some off the top.

"The ocean is just behind those buildings. That's why they're all running here. They run along the seawall." Riki paused. "So, what kind of job do you want to get?"

"I dunno. I worked at a gas station and a café back home."

"Are you going to use Sam's address on your resumé? It would probably help you get a job."

"Yeah, they said I could."

"So all you need is a phone number?"

"Yeah. Sam said I could use their private number, but a pager would help me reply a lot faster. That run-in Sam had with their dad was awful. I'm kind of hoping they find some-where else to live while they finish school."

"Messages can be tough here, too," Riki said, checking to make sure the sliding glass door was closed. "Kim has up days and down days. If they go too far either way, it's hard for them to deal with anyone else's shit. Not to mention that every few months Andy ends up drunk, or worse. It usually takes a cou-ple of weeks for them to get back on the program. Not the fastest for me if I want to return messages that are left here."

"Are you scared of either of them?" I asked.

"No. I've seen a lot of people hit bottom, and neither of them is the type to get mean. They just need their space, so I stay pretty quiet or go somewhere else for a while."

"When did you move in here?"

"After I broke up with my ex a couple months ago. I lived with them and their parents and it got super awkward. I stayed with Sam for a while, and then Kim offered me the spare room. Meeka said they were cool with me moving in, too. They've never had the easiest relationship with their mom."

"It's funny how everyone can stand other people's fucked-up parents more than their own. I mean, as long as they're not too fucked up ..." I let my words trail off before I disappeared down the dark hole of thinking about my own parents and how there was zero possibility of one of my friends ever meeting them.

"Yeah. Even when I lived with my mom as a kid, I was always having to find my own food and look out for myself."

"Sucks," I said, touching Riki's hand. I half hoped some of their toughness would rub off on me.

"What really sucks is Sam's dad," Riki said, looking at our hands touching without making a move to either hold mine or pull away.

I almost pulled away but then decided that Riki was the type to move their hand if they wanted to.

"Yeah. I don't know what to do."

"There's nothing we can do. Until Sam's eighteen, the cops will bring them back home if their dad wants them to. Sometimes their dad lets them leave for a couple of months, but then they always change their mind and want Sam back."

"You're not really your own person until you're eighteen, I guess. Growing up felt like an eternity to me."

"What are you going to do now that you're free?" Riki grinned, trying to lighten the mood, and grabbed my hand in an almost-handshake.

"I don't know. Get a job. Maybe look for some shows to play, like I did in Alberta. I really want to be a musician. Like tour and make albums."

"I bet you can do all of that here." Riki squeezed my hand.

"I hope so," I said, looking up at the sky.

"Hey, Kim's really cool, and I know they wouldn't mind if you stayed here for a while. With me. So, you can if you want to."

I blushed, surprised. "I am feeling pretty freaked out about Sam's dad. I don't think I'd be able to sleep there. Plus, it'd be easier for Sam to run away again if I'm not there ..."

"Great! I'll tell Kim later today. We can go get you a pager downtown, and then bring your stuff up here."

I bought a used pager for twenty-five dollars at a store on Granville Street. It only cost five dollars a month, so I prepaid for a year. As I handed over some of my savings, I reminded myself that I was doing it to get a job. It would pay for itself soon. When I picked my new number I forgot to ask for a funny one that spelled something, like 604-CHEETOS. But just having a pager and getting to pick my first phone number was novelty enough. I started walking a little differently as soon as I put it on my belt, like a gun in its holster.

When we got to Sam's building their bike was outside. Sam and Ocean were upstairs in the kitchen, sitting on the same side of the table, having toast and coffee.

"Hey, you two!" they chimed when Riki and I walked in.

"Hey," I said, smiling, and showed them my new pager.

"Whoa. Matching pagers. Nice!" Sam said, laughing.

"Thanks! I'm going to start looking for a job. Do you mind if I print out some resumés and use your address?"

"Sure. The printer's in the library. I'll take you after we finish breakfast," Sam said.

"Do you have Word?"

Sam nodded. I headed down the hall, relieved to see that no one else was home. I rifled through my backpack and pulled out a floppy disk with my name on it in ballpoint pen. I went back to the kitchen and set it on the table.

"Riki says you're going to stay with them now," Sam said with a smile.

"Yeah," I said, blushing.

"Sounds like a plan. Make sure we still see you lots though, okay?"

Sam had set out a coffee for me without asking. It was starting to feel like we'd known each other a long time.

My plan was simple: find a street I liked and walk down it handing out resumés.

I put my pager on vibrate so it wouldn't interrupt my job search. Copies of my resumé, which now had Sam's address and my new number on it, were in a folder in my backpack. Sam had some new kind of printer, so I didn't have to rip off the edges of the paper and the letters didn't have those lines through the ink. The first street I chose was Davie, where I went into every café, grocery store, video store, restaurant, and bar from Granville to the beach and asked if they were hiring. I skipped the stores with jock straps and underwear in the windows because they made me feel shy. I had put on my best pair of jeans, and I smiled as much as I could without making weird jokes. All the salespeople and managers were friendly. When I hit Sunset Beach I got on a bus back to Granville.

Riki met me at the corner of Davie and Granville and we got on a bus to Commercial Drive. The bus went down Granville, filled up with suits at the SkyTrain station, and then turned east onto Hastings. After a few blocks a person with a boom box on their shoulder got on and sat down at the back of the bus. They sang the entire chorus of "Tainted Love" with fiery conviction. But none of the suits on the bus so much as moved their heads towards the sound. It was like the person was a ghost to them.

It was a sunny day, but a lot of the buildings along Hastings Street were covered in moss or a black ooze that seemed to live in any crack it could get into. As the bus stopped at Main Street, Riki said, "That's the Carnegie Library." They pointed at a beautiful old sandstone building with round turrets and green copper domes. The crowd outside was so big it seemed like there were more people than sidewalk.

"You can go get books there?" I asked.

"Yeah, and there's a lot of cool programs and a kitchen upstairs where you can get dinner for two dollars," Riki said. "I go there a lot at the end of the month, when I start running out of money. The food's pretty good, and they have dessert!"

"Sounds amazing." I'd never actually asked Riki if they had a job.

The bus driver seemed to be invested in boarding the bus quickly. As soon as someone tried to engage them in a discussion about how they didn't have bus fare, the driver would just wave them in. Once everyone (with or without fare) was on, the doors closed and the bus lurched forward with a hiss.

"Are all these buses electric?" I asked Riki.

"If they have those two cables on the back," they said. "Some of them aren't. Like the ones that go all the way out to the suburbs."

I heard the electrical poles clack as we turned onto Commercial Drive.

"Let's get off at the next stop," Riki suggested, and I got up and went to the door early. I liked holding on when a bus stopped—it kind of felt like I was weightless for a second.

We got out right onto a park, where there were people hacky-sacking and lots of others sitting in circles. Punks and hippies, mostly. It reminded me of high school.

"Do you want to sit down for a bit?" Riki asked.

"Sure."

We found a spot that was away from everyone. I sat on the grass and put my backpack off to the side.

"So, do you think you'd like this neighbourhood?" Riki asked.

"It seems chill," I said. "And I want to get a job before my money runs out."

"Okay, well, they're pretty friendly to queer people on this street," Riki said. "Davie is where a lot of rich gays live, but Commercial Drive is more for everyone else, if you know what I mean. People without money."

I nodded. It hadn't really dawned on me that I didn't have money, but the fact was that all the money I had I'd made myself, and there wasn't going to be any more coming from anywhere else. Especially since I didn't buy lottery tickets. I knew that kind of luck wasn't on my side. Once, when I'd turned eighteen, my uncle took me to play the video lottery terminal machines in a bar. My uncle couldn't reach the coin slot from his wheelchair, so I put the coins in while they pressed the buttons. That day was so fun, even though we didn't win anything. I wouldn't ever want to gamble alone. It wouldn't be the same.

I put out the cigarette I no longer remembered lighting. "Well, I better go find some money, then."

I did the same routine as on Davie Street and went into every business I thought might hire me: pet stores, coffee shops, and places that sold bright hair dye and smelled like incense. Every time I came out of a store, Riki was there waiting for me, and we would walk the next ten steps together before I went into another one.

We had walked at least five blocks when I saw a business I couldn't figure out. It was called Vicious Cycle. It was two storefronts wide and had plastic tables in the front.

"It's a café and a laundromat," Riki told me when I hesitated before going in.

"Ohhh," I said. "I'll be right back."

My pile of resumés was getting thin in my hand. I hoped my pager would buzz soon with a message asking me to come in for an interview.

As I walked past the empty tables, I could smell the fabric softener in the spinning dryers in the room on the other side. The person at the cash had black Bettie Page hair and red lipstick.

"Hi, I'm looking for a job and I was wondering if you're hiring right now."

Bettie looked at me without any expression, which made my heart speed up. "Can I see?" they said, gesturing towards my little pile of resumés.

"Sure," I said, accidentally handing them the whole pile.

They perused my resumé for at least a minute and even flipped it over. I couldn't tell what they were thinking.

"So you're from Calgary?"

"Yes, I am."

"I like prairie people. They're hard workers. I'm from Winnipeg. I'm Sharon."

I didn't know what to say back.

"And you worked in a café there?"

"Yes, for a year," I said, hoping my words matched the numbers on the piece of paper.

"Okay. You can have a training shift on Monday, and if that goes well, you can work here."

"Great! What time on Monday?"

"Three p.m. work for you?"

"Sure."

"I'll take one of these so I have your number." Sharon glanced at my pager quizzically but then seemed to make peace with it.

"Okay! See you then!" I said and half ran out of the store.

Riki was sitting on one of the plastic chairs out front, smoking, but stood up when they saw me. I must have been grinning from ear to ear.

"Guess what," I said, not waiting for a guess. "I got a job! I have a trial shift on Monday."

"That's so awesome!" Riki said, clapping me on the back.

We started walking along Commercial again, and I jammed the rest of my resumés into my backpack, not too worried about wrinkling them. I was elated. Once I got an apartment, I would be as set up in Vancouver as I'd been in Calgary.

"Are you hungry?" Riki asked.

"Yeah, a bit."

"Do you have a couple bucks?"

"Yeah, I do."

"You want to get some dollar pizza?"

"Pizza for a dollar?"

"Yeah."

I had never heard of pizza that cheap before. I could see cement SkyTrain tracks ahead of us and hear the low rumble of the train every so often from above. As we were about to walk over a bridge I saw some posters that said *Save Grandview Cut*.

I gestured at them, and Riki said, "This is Grandview Cut. They want to build the new SkyTrain tracks through here."

We stopped in the middle of the bridge and hung our heads over the side. The tops of the trees came up level with the sidewalk. It was like a subterranean forest down there. There was one railway track running through the centre and a lot of garbage, a few shopping carts, and some old mattresses people had tossed.

I pulled my head back up. "It's pretty cool down there."

"Yeah, but there's not much you can do once the city decides it wants something. During Expo 86 they trucked a whole bunch of people away from Main and Hastings to try to make the city look how they wanted it to. That's why so many folks live up this way now. If they treat people like that, imagine how they treat nature."

I shuddered, thinking about people getting rounded up and moved from where they lived. That's what a lot of people in Alberta said they wanted to do with queer people. Put them on an island and blow it up or something.

We crossed the bridge to a pizza place on Commercial Drive and each picked out a slice. Riki put so many chilli peppers all over theirs it would have burned my mouth off. We stood on the sidewalk, munching away quietly.

CHAPTER 7

It was noon the next day when we woke up in Kim's spare room, with fresh empties around the bed. It was Saturday and I didn't start work until Monday. I still had some savings and I'd stopped worrying about spending money.

After the pizza yesterday, Riki and I had gone back downtown to Sam's. I borrowed Sam's BMX so that Riki and I could get around the city without paying for transit every time we wanted to go somewhere. Sam hugged me for a long time before we loaded all my stuff into a taxi that zipped across the Burrard Street Bridge to deposit us at the co-op.

Now, Riki turned sideways and leaned against the wall with their legs over mine. "Do you want to go on a longer bike ride today? We could go to Wreck Beach. It's a nude beach."

I'd never been to a nude beach. I thought they were only in France or something. "Sure," I said.

"Should we pick up more beer, or maybe some whiskey?"

"I have that big bottle in my backpack," I said.

We took our time getting up, pulling on our shorts with our wallets on chains and our keys attached to our belt loops. We each drank two cups of coffee, sipping them on the couch, then made some eggs and toast and ate them looking out onto False Creek. Afterwards, I smoked two or three cigarettes. We didn't talk a lot because we'd been up all night talking about anything that came into our heads. Now my head was pounding a bit, but I knew it would stop soon enough when I took a sip of whiskey.

We went outside and unlocked our bikes. We'd been really careful with Sam's bike, using two locks. One to lock it to Riki's bike and the bike rack, and the other looped through the frames and front wheels of both bikes.

"People will steal your front tire here," Riki had told me.

"Let's go down Broadway," Riki said, lifting their leg up over their bike. "There's that one hill, but after that there's way less than on the other routes."

We stood straight up on our pedals to push off. I had been more into skateboarding than biking in Calgary, but I liked pushing down hard on this bike to get momentum. The small bike was easier to manoeuvre than bigger ones. Broadway was a busy street, so we stuck to the sidewalk, weaving around people and apologizing early to alert them when we had to make a fast move to get around them from behind.

The exhilaration of the ride wore off sometime later when the gas stations and stores seemed to be repeating themselves. I started to feel that particular kind of exhaustion that comes with not knowing a journey's end point. My legs burned when I pedalled in a standing position, and my butt felt bruised from the tiny seat. Still, I followed Riki dutifully, trying not to complain or ask if we were there yet. I would take breaks from the painful seat by gliding with my legs extended until they hurt too much, and then go back to sitting down.

Eventually, the city blocks changed into the manicured green lawns of University Boulevard and the smell of the ocean grew stronger.

Riki turned around and shouted, "Let's lock our bikes at the university. They'll be safer here."

The campus reminded me of the day a lot of my friends started university in Calgary and I went to see some bands play at a welcome concert. Everyone always says that if you go to university, you'll get a really good job. That night, before the concert, I was working at a gas station, wondering if I had made a big mistake as I squeegeed car windows. I didn't have a real plan. I was just going to sing and hope it got me somewhere, but I always felt too young when I was looking for gigs. It seemed like there was something about me that made it hard for people to take me seriously. When I played shows they always went well, but I mostly played at the café where I worked and at the Mermaid downtown. It had started to seem like a circle after a while. The gas station, then a show. Then a new job at a café, and a show.

Sam's suggestion that I try out Vancouver was like a lightning bolt. That was where the Scrappy Bitch Tour people were from: Kinnie Starr, Veda Hille, and Oh Susanna. Leaving Calgary seemed like taking a chance, but so was singing at all. I wondered what my life would be like in ten, fifteen, or twenty years. Would I be doing what I wanted to do, or would I be far behind everyone who went to university?

I wondered what my life would be like in ten, fifteen, or twenty years.

"Okay, this is it!" Riki said, pulling me out of my deep thoughts. "There are four hundred and seventy-three stairs down, and it feels like more coming back up."

The path to the beach was a quick drop-off into the forest. We started down the wooden stairs, and as we walked into the canopy, I could smell the wet, fertile soil mixed with old broken twigs. Like the bike ride out here, the journey felt endless, but eventually the last stair gave way to a sandy beach strewn with logs. As promised, there were naked people everywhere.

I was hit by a feeling of soaring freedom, quickly followed by the realization that I wasn't capable of being nude on a beach. I started to panic. I thought about the many times I'd gotten in trouble for running around with my shirt off when I was young. But it had taken us so long to get here that the sun was getting low now, and I figured it would be too cold for nudity soon. I could just wait it out. I spotted a couple of other clothed people and felt a bit better. Riki didn't take any clothes off either, except their socks and shoes. I could relax.

We picked a log to lean against, stretched our feet out towards the water, and passed the bottle of whiskey back and forth for a while, sipping silently.

"Do you come here a lot?" I finally asked.

"Yeah. It kind of reminds me of home. I mean, not the water, which is really fucking cold, or the way anything looks, really. But the people here are a lot more open than they are at the top of the stairs."

"Do you ever take your clothes off and swim or anything?"

"I might swim if it was really, really hot, but even then I'd probably leave some of my clothes on. No one here would care, though. It's a real do-what-you-feel place. Sometimes it's nice to just be around that."

"Yeah. I've never been anywhere like this."

I leaned back, closed my eyes, and let the sun warm my eyelids. If not for the odd sound of a wave or footstep in the sand, it would have been easy to forget where I was.

A voice next to us jolted my eyes open. "Hey, do you want to buy a samosa?" The person grinned at us, completely naked except for a large fanny pack.

"We're good, but thanks," Riki said, and the seller walked away.

"They're always selling samosas here at this time of day," Riki said with a twinkle in their eye. I could tell they thought it was great.

We got back into watching the ocean. It sparked more orange as the sun changed colour on its way down. Pretty soon the sun was setting, and Riki and I inched closer together as it got colder.

"Let's move," Riki said. "People sometimes build a fire over there when the sun goes down."

As we walked, the steady thumping noise I had been hearing for a while began to make sense. A tall naked person with an axe was trying to hack a piece of wet driftwood in half against the grain. The tree was waterlogged and it wasn't going well. As the axe met the wood I could see each ripple on their body, even though I was trying not to.

People were gathering driftwood for the fire, so we grabbed some pieces, too. It was getting colder and a lot of people were putting their clothes back on. Riki didn't know any of them, but they were really good at saying, "Hey, how's it going?" and setting people at ease with some light conversation. I was still getting comfortable, so I mostly said nothing, like the old trees around us. My steady sips from the bottle of whiskey helped me relax, and I slowly started talking to people. We talked about almost nothing, but I could feel my face shining with contentment.

As it grew darker, the fire got bigger and more people crowded around. Riki told me there were some creeps at Wreck Beach, so they stuck close to me all night. We sat with the front of our bodies glowing orange and our backs in full eclipse. Log after log was thrown onto the fire, and we howled if a lot of sparks danced up towards the sky as the wood shifted. Someone pulled out a beat-up, sticker-covered guitar and started warming up the jam with Bob Marley's "Stir It Up." The familiarity of the music made me feel at home, and I joined in happily. This was my home now, I told myself.

I quietly sang along with all the songs, but I never took the guitar when it was being passed around. After a few songs the person who'd been chopping wood naked grabbed the guitar and said, "You're all going to love this song because it's a true story."

The singer started thrumming so wildly on the strings, I wondered if they were going to break. The song had a very long intro at a rapid tempo. I was waiting for the first verse to start, but the song really had only one line.

The person paused dramatically and bellowed, "My girlfriend has a pussy. My girlfriend has a pussy. My girlfriend has a pussy like a sleeping bag."

I was immediately sickened and scared, but a lot of people around the fire grinned. The unwelcome and familiar scrape of feeling unsafe clawed down my back. I could tell I wasn't the only one affected that way. A few people pulled their towels up over their bodies like they were battening down the hatches against this storm. The jam had just flown off a cliff like a van that's trying to jump a raised bridge and misses, falling out of sight.

I shot Riki a look that said it was time-to-go o'clock.

Riki leaned over and said, not so quietly, "This song fucking sucks. Let's go hang out over there."

I noticed how drunk I was when I stumbled as we started walking down the dark beach. The song was as endless as it was meaningless as it was creepy. It got quieter as we moved away, but every time it was about to wind down, the few fans would yell, "One more time!"

"Ugh," I said. "I hate when people use their power, like that guitar in that person's hand, to throw around abuse."

The claws of the past had let go of me, and I was back in the present, ready to follow them anywhere.

"I feel the same way," Riki said. "I didn't know what to do. I pictured wrestling the guitar away from them, but then I worried I'd fall right on top of them."

"Ewwwww!" I screamed, and we both chuckled.

Riki had lightened the heaviness in my body. The claws of the past had let go of me, and I was back in the present, ready to follow them anywhere.

"It's pretty late," Riki said. "I don't think we should try to bike home. We can sleep on the beach, if you're cool with that."

I flopped down; the sand still felt warm. "Yeah, that's cool with me."

We lay down on our sides facing each other. While we were falling asleep holding hands, Riki started to whisper stories about their life to me.

"My grandma was a model in California. Nothing big, but they had some roles ... Sometimes I'd live with my grandma. Sometimes I'd go out on my own ... When I was fifteen, I fell off a roof at a party. I don't really remember how. I broke my hip. That's why I limp sometimes now. It still hurts a lot."

I stayed silent, wondering if I'd noticed a limp. I tried not to notice things people didn't tell me about because I figured they'd tell me if they wanted me to know. Riki seemed like someone who didn't appreciate people prying into their business. I squeezed their hand and let the whiskey pull me into sleep.

CHAPTER 8

I showed up for my first day of work at three p.m. on Monday.
The laundromat was half full, and most of the washers and
dryers were spinning. On the café side, people were drinking
coffee, reading books, and chatting.

"This is Keith," Sharon said, introducing me to the almost-
seven-foot-tall person standing next to them at the counter.
"They're going to train you today. You got this, Keith?"

"Yep, no worries," Keith said, putting their hands in their
pockets and standing up straighter.

Sharon grabbed some keys and said, "Good luck!" before
heading out.

Keith turned to the till. "So you've worked in a café before?"

I nodded.

"Laundromat?"

"No."

"Okay. Usually there are two of us on at a time. Our first
priority is to make sure the cash machine is covered. It's not

good to leave this area alone for too long. Things tend to happen. That's also why all of our tips are swimming in this coloured water here. If anyone tries to run off with the tip jar, they get doused and dyed."

I nodded again and looked at the bowl of water with the tips in it like I understood what they were talking about. That had never happened at the café in Alberta.

"The quarters are locked in here." Keith took a key out of their pocket and unlocked the drawer underneath the till. There were rolls and rolls of coins as well as a plastic yogurt container full of loose quarters.

"You sell someone quarters, you ring it onto the till here and put their cash into the till. Be careful to make sure you get the numbers right when you enter them. Sharon keeps a pretty close watch on the quarters. Now, food, coffee, and drinks go through the till as well. The items are all here on the buttons, as well as sizes to enter after if you need to. See: *Coffee. Large.*" Keith pecked the buttons. "Then total to add the tax ... Oh! We only take cash here. There's an ATM in the convenience store that way and a bank at Commercial and First." They gestured towards the intersection a few blocks away.

"We also do people's laundry for them. Here are the buttons for a load to wash and a load to dry. You know how to do laundry?"

"Yep."

Before I moved out of Mom's duplex, my bed was in the unfinished basement right next to the washer and dryer. The sound of the machines made me feel vaguely sleepy. I had a lot of time to learn how to wash clothes in that basement, especially since I'd bought a bunch of boxer shorts at the Army & Navy at Marlborough Mall and didn't feel like having a discussion about it with my mother.

"Great. We wash it, we dry it, we fold it, and we put it into one of these blue garbage bags with a tag. There's a load in the dryer now you can fold in a bit." Keith went on, "Okay, you know espresso drinks? One shot, twelve ounce. Two shots, sixteen. Two shots, twenty, unless they ask for more."

It was the same at the café I'd worked at before I moved.

"Milk's in this fridge. Coffee grinder is here. Drip coffee machine. Beans are already measured in the filters. I'll show you how to do that later."

Keith scratched their chin, not bothered by the fact that I hadn't said anything in a while. "Okay, what else? Oh, yeah. Food. Sharon loves Mexican food, so that's mostly what we have. We do our own nachos. Cheese, olives, peppers, and microwave for two minutes. We do a lot of our own prep here. Have you ever cut these up before?" Keith asked.

"Jalapenos?" I pronounced it with a hard *J* sound.

"Nooo, *h*alapenos," Keith said, pulling one out of the bigger refrigerator.

"*H*alapenos," I said.

Keith nodded. "Slice them in half like this, cut off the stems, and take out the seeds and white stuff in the middle like this."

I leaned in to make sure I could see what Keith was doing.

"Then dice them like this. Now you try," Keith said. "Oh, really important! Remember to wash the hot pepper oils off your hands with soap, or when you go to the bathroom it'll be like a fire in your pants. Like serious hot pants."

Somehow I knew this had happened to Keith before. I looked at them quizzically, and then realized they thought I was the sort of person who went to the bathroom standing up. Keith quickly realized they might have made a mistake.

"Oh! Sorry, dude. I was thinking that you were ... I mean. Don't rub your eyes or anything after cutting them. They are super hot!"

"That's cool," I said. "It happens a lot."

Keith looked out the window for a moment. I turned and noticed the light outside had turned a deeper orange.

Keith started talking again. "We don't really have dinner rushes here. It's more like a steady stream. People do their laundry when they can and get food and drinks while they wait."

A buzzer went off in the other room and Keith said, "Watch the front."

Anything can happen here. Stay alert! I reminded myself as they disappeared into the other room.

Keith came back with a basket full of laundry and dumped it on a large wooden table against a wall. "All right. Wash the jalapeno off your hands, and then you can fold these. Here's the blue garbage bag. The tag is tied onto the basket."

I went to the washroom and carefully soaped up my hands twice. Back at the table, I resisted the urge to push my face into the pile of warm laundry, like I used to do as a child. I carefully folded items the way I had been taught. The rhythm made me forget I was nervous about my first day. After each fold I smoothed out the fabric so the cloth would lie as flat as possible. When I was finished there were neat piles of all the different clothes. I lifted the largest items into the bottom of the blue bag first. I made them as flat as possible on the bottom and put the looser stuff on top. I knotted the bag and then tied the tag around the knot.

"Looks good. You can put it on that chair," Keith said as I came back to the counter, holding the bag straight out from my body so I wouldn't disturb the balance. I lowered it carefully onto the empty chair.

After that I made all of the coffees and meals people ordered. I gave out quarters and put cash and the notes about quarters in the till. After a while, there was a lull in people coming in, which gave me a chance to look around. I noticed a baseball bat leaning against the counter where it met the wall.

Keith saw me looking at it. "That's in case any of these dudes get fresh with the people who work the late shifts here. The person you replaced was eight months pregnant when they chased some jerk out a couple of weeks ago. For good reason!"

At the end of my shift Keith showed me how to cash out and then dried off our tips on a towel. They exchanged the coins for bills and handed me a blue five-dollar bill, two loonies, and a quarter. I smiled and shoved them into my pocket.

"Looks like you're scheduled to work next on Wednesday, from three p.m. until close. I'll be working with you again. You can go now if you want, and I'll lock up."

"Cool. Thanks!" I scooped up my jacket and walked out into the night.

Commercial Drive looked different in the dark. In Calgary, the few people who were out at night often proved to be dangerous. All the stores and cafés on the Drive were closed, but there were still a lot of folks around. I started walking towards Broadway to get the bus to False Creek. I stopped on the bridge and leaned over the edge to look down into the Grandview Cut, where I could barely make out the gleam of the railway tracks at the bottom. Some movement caught my eye and I saw a person crouched almost at the top of the cut, next to where the bridge touched the street. They had one shoe off and were pushing a needle in between their toes. That sight was new for me. Even though I was learning not to judge what people did, it held my eyes until they looked up at me. I felt my face turn red and whispered, "Sorry," before taking off at breakneck speed.

When I got back to the co-op, Kim and Andy were watching TV and Riki was in the bedroom. I sat on the bed and they said, "My friends who live on Pender and Woodland had an apartment come free in their building. It's close to your job, a two-bedroom, and the rent is seven-fifty. We could even get a roommate."

"That would be super cheap," I said.

"It's available now. Like, if we had the damage deposit we could move in right away."

"Can we go see it?" I asked.

"I already looked at it while you were at work. It's old but decent. I talked to the caretaker of the building and they're cool with us moving in."

"Okay. How much is the damage deposit?" I asked.

"One month's rent. I even know someone who might want to move in with us. So we'd just have to cover five hundred dollars."

I thought about my bank account. "I have five hundred dollars."

"You do? That's awesome," Riki said.

"When can we move in?"

"Tomorrow. Are you working?"

"No. I don't work until Wednesday."

"Perfect! Let's go tell Kim."

Kim and Andy beamed at us. "You're going to like living over there," Kim said, patting Riki's knee.

"Yeah. I'll still have three hundred dollars left over from my cheque every month after rent." Riki was grinning as they spoke.

We went back to the bedroom to pack up. I hadn't pulled much out of my backpack since I got there the other day, but Riki had tons of stuff.

"We'll probably need to get one of those air mattress beds," Riki said. "There's an Army & Navy on Hastings. We could score a cheap one there."

I nodded. I had seen the store from the bus.

"The apartment's right by Value Village, so if we need dishes or anything we can get them there," Riki said.

This was going to be my first time starting a home with someone.

This was going to be my first time starting a home with someone.

In the morning we said goodbye to Kim and Andy and promised to visit for tea soon. We took a van taxi with all of our stuff to the apartment. It was actually two buildings on the corner with a small corridor between them. They were practically attached, but one entrance was on Woodland and the other was on Pender. Two exact copies, rotated and facing different streets. We locked the bikes together out front in the usual way.

There was no buzzer at the front door, so Riki just pounded on it until the caretaker came down. They looked like Beetlejuice, with straight white hair and a glint in their eye. We stashed our stuff in the front entrance and followed Beetlejuice up three flights of stairs to an apartment at the very top of the building. There was cheap grey carpet everywhere except the bathroom and kitchen, which had old brownish linoleum that curled in the corners. It wasn't clean or new, but I wasn't really expecting that. I gave a cheque for the damage deposit to Beetlejuice, who said they didn't mind if we moved in a few days early and paid rent when Riki's cheque came in at Kim's place. When Beetlejuice left, Riki and I just stood there for a moment, grinning at each other.

We walked down Hastings to the Army & Navy department store. I was getting used to the way people would move in every direction as they walked in the Downtown Eastside. One person took off quickly into traffic after an explosive whistle, and a bunch of cars started honking from both directions. *We all live here*, I thought, frowning.

Army & Navy smelled like imitation rubber; it reminded me of the same store back home. Riki and I bought a double air mattress, some cleaning supplies, a washcloth, and a tea towel. The cashier rang us through and put everything into huge thin plastic bags. We each carried two bags and waited for a bus that would take us to the corner of Hastings and Commercial. Walking from the bus stop to the apartment, I felt the handles of the bags start to cut into my hands. I didn't complain, though, because Riki wasn't complaining.

We dumped the bags on the living room floor and then took turns blowing up the air mattress in our room. Kim had given us some pillows and sheets, and I had a sleeping bag I could unzip to make a double blanket.

"Emily will be here soon," Riki said. "They'll give you two-fifty for the damage deposit."

We lay side by side on the air mattress, staring at the ceiling. There were some brown water marks, and my eyes traced a crack that went from the middle of the ceiling to one of the corners.

After a few minutes Riki's pager buzzed. They stood up and hung their head out our open window. "Oh, hi!" they called down, and then dropped a set of keys down three storeys onto the grass. "Let yourself in!"

"I left the rest of my stuff in the car," Emily said, walking into the apartment with frizzy hair and tons of bags. "Oh! I have lawn chairs," they said, noticing that there was no furniture in the living room.

"Hi," I said.

"Nice to meet you," Emily said. "I'll be right back with more stuff."

"Do you want some help?" I asked.

"Sure."

Riki didn't come out of the bedroom, so I assumed they needed to rest. I followed Emily down the stairs and propped open the front door of the building with a rock. We walked to their car, which was parked around the corner, and I grabbed a stack of white plastic patio furniture out of the back.

"No table?" I joked.

"I guess we'll have to find one in an alley or something," Emily said.

"Sure." I hefted the lawn chairs up on my stomach and stood on one foot to push the car door closed with the other.

"Chairs!" I announced as I unstacked them in the living room.

Riki bounded out of the bedroom and sprawled in one of them. I went back downstairs to see if I could grab anything else.

Emily was moving out of their parents' house. "My bed's coming tomorrow in my dad's truck," they said, and handed me a sweaty wad of cash that I stashed in my back pocket. Then they went to their room and started unpacking.

A few hours later, the three of us walked to the beer store on Hastings and grabbed enough cheap beer to fill a whole shelf of our fridge. In fact, it was the only thing in our fridge.

Riki and I pulled out our instruments and I leaned against the wall under the window and strummed on my guitar quietly. The other two sat in lawn chairs facing me. The first beers we finished became our ashtrays as we cracked more beers and chatted. The three of us laughed a lot and the many beers made me glow. Riki and I played some music, and it felt good to sing again. It felt like I had everything I needed.

CHAPTER 9

Keith and I both looked a bit bleary-eyed when we started work at the same time the next afternoon. We took turns clearing and wiping the tables and restocking the food prep area.

Keith tried to make conversation during a lull. "So you're from Calgary."

"Yeah, I lived there all my life until now."

"That's cool. I'm from Saskatoon. You're going to love the winters out here. I mean, it rains, but you're not going to get lost in a blizzard walking to your car or have your eyelids freeze shut or anything."

I hadn't really considered a winter without snow. "Are your parents from Saskatoon?" I asked.

"Yep. Old-school. My mom went to high school with Joni Mitchell."

"Holy shit!"

"Yeah. One time my mom was like, 'Three p.m. at the bike racks, Joni! It's on.'"

I chuckled. "Wow. So you like music?"

"I love music. I want to be a producer someday."

"Cool. I love music, too. I've recorded a bit, but only on a four-track."

"It's so fun. Have you ever noticed the power of the humble tambourine?" Keith pointed to a speaker, and I heard the tambourine in the song that was playing. I listened closely until it stopped for part of the song. I waited, and when it came back the song lifted and seemed faster. Or maybe deeper. Like something you really wanted to tap your foot to.

"I see what you mean," I said.

"Yeah, so soon I'll try to find artists to work with."

"So what's a producer do, anyway? Do they run the sound board?"

"Nope. That's the engineer."

"Oh. Right." I put my hands in my pockets.

Out of the corner of my eye I saw a customer at the cash. It was Riki, smiling.

"Hey," they said. "Do you want to go to a thing at the WISE Hall tonight? It's just up the hill from our house. I can meet you there."

"Sounds good."

"It's a queer cabaret thing," Riki said, turning over a flyer on the counter and grabbing a pen to draw a map.

"I get off at nine," I said.

"All right, see you there." Riki winked and walked out the door.

The next customer ordered some nachos. Keith rang them in while I pulled out all the bins of food and opened the big plastic container full of chips.

"Hey, they ordered banana peppers on it, too," Keith called back to me. "They're the orange and yellow ones."

I layered chips and cheese on a plate and used a spoon to scoop out the banana peppers, careful not to dump the liquid on the chips. Then I put the whole thing in the microwave and leaned back against the counter.

"Salsa? Sour cream?" Keith asked.

I leapt back into motion, grabbed two small bowls, filled them to the brim with salsa and sour cream, and put them on another plate with a pile of napkins.

"Perfect. They're right over there. We can take out the order together," Keith said.

The microwave beeped and Keith grabbed the plate and started to fake some sort of official type of walk. I picked up the other plate and followed them, copying their silly gait. They placed the plate on the table between two bike couriers and said, "Your dinner is served."

They chuckled and I put my plate down and almost did a curtsy. Keith and I skittered back to the till together.

"Hey, do you have an email address?" Keith asked.

"No. I never had one because I would have had to share it with my parents," I said.

"Well, there's, like, webmail now. That means it's mobile, so you just log in and it lives online, not on anyone's computer," Keith said. "Anyway, I really want to show you this website. We can wait until it's slow and I'll show you on the café computer. We let people use it for free if they buy stuff here."

"Right on," I said.

Later, Keith typed something into the computer and said, "Check this out."

I leaned into the glowing box and saw tons and tons of pictures of Kenny Rogers—but Kenny looked a bit weird in each of them. "You like Kenny Rogers?" I asked.

"No, check it out. People submit photos of people who look like Kenny Rogers." Keith was holding his breath, trying not to lose himself to laughter.

The people in the photos reminded me a bit of mall Santas who had decided to keep their beards short for the summer.

"The slight variation between the different Kennys makes it fucking hilarious," Keith said. "Like this Kenny is a golfer, and this one works at McDonald's. I don't know, it's just ..."

I glanced up at Keith's towering figure and saw the child-like glee in their eyes. Keith's wholehearted enjoyment of the Kennys finally pulled me into laughter to the point of tears as they scrolled through row after row.

A while later Keith said, "Hey, I think you got off work five minutes ago."

"I love this job!" I said, grabbing my coat and cigarettes.

I walked down Commercial, searching for anyone who looked like Kenny Rogers. There were a few close calls, but no matches.

Soon I hit a sign that said *Adanac. Adanac, Adanac*, I thought. *That's Canada backwards!* I started laughing as I turned up the hill. I eventually came across a park with a bunch of people hanging out in the playground, smoking. It seemed like everyone in Vancouver was like my friends in high school, like the whole city was down to hang out in a playground in the middle of the night or hacky-sack in a park in the middle of the day.

I kept walking until I saw a crowd of people on the side-walk and spilling out into the street. A whole bunch of them looked like Riki. After I checked everyone's face and deter-mined none of them was Riki, I climbed the stairs to the door.

"Five-dollar cover," said a person sitting behind a tall table. They had slicked-back hair and three nose rings.

I pulled my tips out of my pocket and handed over the five. They stamped my wrist with a blue sailor, and then I walked into a long rectangular room with no windows and very little light. It was filled with hundreds of people standing around chatting while music played. I walked to the back of the room and looked at the stage with my hands in my pockets. I'd never seen this many queer people in one place before. I felt myself start to vibrate with excitement, and then I noticed the line to the bar behind me.

"A beer, please," I said to a bartender wearing a white tank top and rainbow suspenders. I handed over some money, making sure to tip them a dollar.

Drink in hand, I felt more purposeful. I walked around the perimeter of the room, scanning for Riki. Finally, when some music started coming from the stage, I decided to let them come to me.

Two people dressed in similar collared shirts and work pants walked out onstage. They both had super-short haircuts that reminded me of when my mother used to shave all our heads in our backyard.

I'd never seen this many queer people in one place before.

"Hey everyone," one of them said. "The show's about to begin."

People gravitated towards the front and got quieter.

"I'm Michael and this is Tom. The first performer we're going to welcome tonight is Drake—or should I say, Slimmmmmmmmm Shadyyyyyyyyyy."

A hysterical scream moved through the crowd as all the lights went out, reminding me of a haunted house. Then it was quiet for a few seconds while lone hoots resounded from different parts of the room. A spotlight ignited and I saw a figure standing statue-like, wearing track pants, sneakers, and a hooded sweatshirt pulled low over their head.

A nasal voice came over the speakers—Eminem's singing, which is more akin to whining. The spotlight came on full blast and Drake started lip-synching into an unplugged microphone. They moved from one side of the stage to the other with a macho gait, machine-gunning the words. They just kept saying their name over and over, but people seemed into it. The crowd pressed closer to the stage and some people were nodding.

Drake pulled their sweatshirt off to reveal a flat chest under a white tank top and slid across the stage on their knees. They lip-synched something about how they had more balls than everyone else. Drake grabbed their crotch and a bunch of people screamed. Then they ripped off their tearaway track pants to reveal a pair of tight underwear with a huge bulge at the front. I'd always wondered why big balls were considered something that would inspire awe. To me, it always seemed like the person going on about the size of theirs was very worried about who they'd be if they didn't have a certain kind of body. It must be scary carrying around your treasured, giant balls in a world where they're so important.

During the final chorus, Drake reached into their underwear to a crescendo of cheers and whistles. The screaming demands that the real Slim Shady stand up grew more intense. Most people were already standing up, but there were no challengers. Drake smiled slyly, looked down, pulled a teddy bear out of their underwear, and tossed it to the back of the crowd. Everyone laughed, and then the song ended and Drake strutted offstage.

Some people in Calgary said Eminem was hateful towards women and flagrantly homophobic. But I had never seen a drag king before, so maybe I didn't really understand. Maybe dressing up like a man meant you had to act like the worst kind of man. No one else seemed upset, so I tried to quiet my brain.

Michael walked back onstage and said, "Drake, everyone! Drag King Drake!"

I felt a tap on my shoulder. When I turned around and saw Riki, I flushed.

"Do you want to go out for a smoke?" they asked.

"Sure!"

We went outside and stood apart from the crowd of other people puffing away.

"Sorry I'm late," Riki said. "I was looking into a job."

"A job? Where?"

"I'll show you when we get home."

"Okay," I said, lacing my fingers though theirs. I put my head on Riki's shoulder and inhaled their scent.

A few minutes later, we went back upstairs to find a person onstage wearing tasselled pasties and a thong. They gestured grandly to the crowd and sat delicately on a cake. I smiled. Then someone rolled them offstage while they straddled the cake, waving. The crowd was roaring.

Riki grabbed us more beer and held me from behind while we watched the rest of the show. Not everything I saw made sense to me. Once in a while Riki would whisper an explanation in my ear, like, "That's fisting," and I would solemnly absorb the information. I couldn't figure out how fisting worked no matter how hard I tried. Maybe I could get a book about it from the library sometime.

The lights went up and Riki said their goodbyes with me in tow. I introduced myself and said goodbye over and over.

I'd never felt so certain about a person in my life.

Riki inspired a playful glint in people, and I felt happy and connected to everyone who felt that way about them.

Outside, we each lit a cigarette, rejoined hands, and let the hill on Adanac Street pull us gently towards home, our shoes softly scuffing the pavement. I wasn't chattering non-stop to deal with my nervousness, the way I had been since I'd met Riki. They smiled at me and squeezed my hand. I'd never felt so certain about a person in my life. I wondered how I'd gotten lucky enough to stumble upon someone so perfect so soon after leaving home. Then I did something rare for me and let go of my worries, feeling my shoulders lower a bit.

"Riki?"

"Yeah."

"Adanac backwards spells Canada," I said and chuckled.

"Youuuuu crackkked the cooooddde," Riki said maniacally. "And now that you know all our secrets ... you have to stay here with me."

Riki pulled me towards them right in the middle of the street and kissed me. We kissed all the way up the three flights of stairs to our apartment. We rolled around on our blow-up mattress, somehow managing not to pop it.

After, we lay still on our backs next to each other, completely naked, and smoked.

"Riki?"

They sort of grunted.

"Um, I felt kind of weird at the show. Like, I love having sex, and I don't mind being naked with you no matter how bad I feel, but do people ever, like, ask permission or warn people if they're going to get naked onstage?"

Riki was quiet for a minute. "No, I don't remember anyone ever asking for anything like that, and I guess folks are scared of being called a prude if they do. This queer scene is kind of harsh—like a contest to see who's the queerest, especially since most of us come from places where we had to hide it or people would try to stamp it out of us."

I stayed silent, wanting to hear more.

"It would be cool to warn people, though," Riki said.

"It would be nice to be able to choose," I said. "Some days things in my brain are fine, but other times it costs me a lot to pretend I'm sooooo queer. I bet there are others who feel the same."

Riki grabbed my hand and nodded. I could see they were going to try to lift the mood. "Okay, but the most important warning we should have gotten tonight will probably haunt me in my dreams ..."

"Yeah?" I asked, wondering what could be more harmful than an unsolicited sex workshop.

"Well, remember that act that rolled out on a cake?"

"Yeah."

"Often there's food backstage for performers or techs or whatever ..." Riki's mouth twitched into a smile. "What if some unsuspecting person somehow missed that act?"

I started shaking with giggles. "Oh shit!" I burst out. "There's a one hundred percent chance someone ate some of that cake!"

"Well, yeah! Also, a lot of people would probably want to eat that cake just because that person sat on it."

Riki exploded with laughter, and I rolled over to bury my face in their neck. I loved the way they smelled. I loved the way they laughed. We were both still laughing when we fell asleep.

CHAPTER 10

When I woke up the next morning Riki was still sleeping, so I reached over gently to my cigarettes on the floor and lit one as quietly as I could. I had the day off. I picked up my pager and saw it was eleven a.m. The seagulls outside were in full swing, fighting over something in front of the building. I lay on my back and blew a cloud of smoke over our heads.

Riki stirred. "Hey, we should get some dishes today," they said, rolling over. "We can't keep eating out of our hands. I think I saw a mouse last night when I went to the bathroom, and some cockroaches. It would be good to keep the crumbs off the floor." They snagged the lit cigarette out of my hand and took a slow drag, not handing it back right away.

"Sure," I said. "Where do you want to get them?"

"We can go see what they have at Value Village," Riki replied, taking another puff and passing my cigarette back.

"Okay. I'll go make some coffee."

I stood up and looked for my shorts. In the kitchen, I made a mental note to sweep up later and then carefully teetered back to our room with two steaming cups. Riki was sitting up but not out of bed yet. I put a cup next to them, sat back down on the air mattress, and leaned against the wall.

"Do you think the mouse would come in here?" I asked.

"Nah, they go where the food is. Same with cockroaches. They like the water, so they'll both just hang out in the kitchen and the bathroom. Mice will leave eventually if they don't find anything to eat. Cockroaches are different. Once they're in a building, you can't really get rid of them. So I guess we just have to get used to them. At least they're small here. Not like in California."

I tried to make my peace with the cockroaches, but it wasn't happening. I felt a crawling sensation on my arm and jumped, almost spilling both our coffees.

"I smell sugar!" I exclaimed as we walked down Hastings.

"Yeah, that's the doughnut factory. I heard they have an unlocked Dumpster that's full of doughnuts that don't pass the test. My friend told me they found it once and ate a bunch and had a doughnut fight!"

"It smells really good." My stomach growled as we walked another block to some traffic lights. "Ewww, what the fuck is that stink?" This wasn't doughnuts; it smelled like death itself.

"That's the chicken factory." Riki pointed at a building with really high walls around it. "See." They pointed to the ground and I noticed tons of small feathers caught in the grass.

I covered my nose and mouth and yelled another muffled, "Ewwwwwwwww!"

"If we move faster, we can get away from the smell!" Riki took off across the street full-tilt as the walk sign started beeping.

We ran up the hill as fast as we could, but the reek of the chickens meeting their deaths seemed to be faster. At the top of the hill I saw the familiar red sign. I'd bought a lot of my clothes at Value Village in Calgary until one of my exes made fun of me and told me I should shop at Mountain Equipment Co-op instead. They'd gone to some private school where they could watch Olympic rowers practise on the lake. They were friends with all the cool kids in Calgary.

Inside, Riki zigged left, grabbing a cart, and then zagged right, with purpose. I followed a little less gracefully, trying to keep up as they pushed the cart fast and turned a corner. Then I saw the usual shelves covered in dishes, lamps without shades, shades without lamps (fewer of those), coffee mugs, and wooden salad bowls. There weren't many water glasses, so we agreed to drink out of mugs. The plates and bowls were plentiful, but didn't match. Some of the pans looked like a person had tried to cut their steak right in them, but we found one that seemed functional. We also found some aluminum pots, and one even had a lid. There were two somewhat sharp steak knives we decided would be good for cutting pretty much anything.

Then we rolled the whole heaping cart over to checkout. The red-vested employee rang the dishes through without looking up, wrapped them in newspaper, and put them in giant white plastic bags. Riki took two and I wrapped my arms around the heaviest one. I paid something like forty dollars and we went back out onto the street.

When we got home we piled the bags near the kitchen sink. Riki told me they weren't quite punk enough to eat off used dishes without washing them first.

Emily was in the living room, looking out the window thoughtfully and blowing smoke rings, few of which were successful.

"Dishes!" Riki screeched, waving a freshly unwrapped mug into the room.

"Sweet! I was getting pretty tired of drinking water out of that old Slurpee cup in my room." Emily laughed. "Oh, hey, I called Mike and Angie, and they're going to come over later."

"Nice! I haven't seen them since I stopped going to class when I finished my credits early," Riki said.

"Angie was having a pretty rough time last week," Emily said.

"Yeah, we talked on the phone. They were hearing voices and shit," Riki called from the kitchen. "I told them to maybe take a break from acid for a while."

"Well, I think they did and they're feeling a bit better now."

"That's good!" Riki said.

I lit a cigarette and sat down in a lawn chair in the living room. Emily might have been ignoring me. I wasn't sure. Neither of us spoke, and I didn't know why or what to say. I remembered my guitar and got it from my room and leaned it against the wall in the living room.

After a few minutes, Riki came out of the kitchen with some wet spots on the front of their shirt. "It will be great to see Angie and Mike!" they said, jolting Emily and me out of our silence.

"How do you all know each other?" I asked.

"We all went to a program for dropouts to help us finish high school. We graduate in June, but I finished my work last month," Riki said, chuckling. "Hey, are you hungry?"

"Yeah." It was, like, two p.m.

"Let's go up to the Drive and get some breakfast."

"Okay."

"You coming?" Riki asked Emily.

"Nah, I'm good," Emily said.

We walked up the gentle hill of the Drive, past Nick's Spaghetti House to Venables Street, and then crossed at the

lights and went into the Skylight Restaurant. The inside smelled like old grease and looked as if it had never been renovated in all its years, with bright red vinyl seats and tables where plates and elbows had rubbed the enamel off glacially. Riki placed their elbows in two of the worn-out spots and picked up the menu. We decided we'd both have the $3.50 breakfast, with two eggs, bacon, and white toast.

While we waited for our food, Riki took my hand and put two keys in it. "I'm going to go see a friend about that job this afternoon," they said. "Do you mind going back to the apartment by yourself after we eat?"

"Sure, I can do that."

"Cool."

We sprayed bright red ketchup all over our food to give it a colour other than yellow and brown. I stopped noticing the grease smell in the restaurant as soon as I started eating. After we cleaned our plates, I paid and Riki jumped on a bus downtown.

As I walked back down the hill, the streets were quiet for midafternoon. When I got home Emily's bedroom door was closed, but I figured they were in there because I could smell cigarette smoke.

I grabbed a mug of water, wishing we had some beer, and went into the living room. I picked up my guitar and tried to sit in one of the lawn chairs but quickly realized the arms wouldn't allow me to hold the instrument comfortably. I picked a spot on the floor and played some of my songs—some that were slow, and some that people seemed to like. Then I started strumming random chords to try to write a new song. Some of the chords started to work with each other, and I began to hum and look for words, but none came easily. I noticed that the bright afternoon light had angled and turned golden when a patch made its way onto my face.

I leaned my guitar against the wall and went to refill my water. I looked out the window across the city skyline and noticed a giant billboard between here and downtown. It showed the gargantuan head of an infant with an impossible smile and hollow eyes. All it said was *The Gap*. I thought about the Downtown Eastside, the neighbourhood between our apartment and the skyscrapers, the blocks that were always teeming with activity any hour of the day. Did advertisers think people there needed to buy their children miniature khakis and checked shirts? Even the adults around here didn't dress like that. These thoughts made me feel tired, so I headed to our room to lie down.

I woke up in the dark when I heard a bunch of people coming in the front door and my skin prickled. Then I picked out Riki's voice and relaxed. I got out of bed slowly. I'd been lying in it fully clothed. I put my pager back in my pocket, even though

I had a job now and the only other people with the number were Sam and Riki. Emily's door was closed and the light was off. I could feel my hair was standing up at the front, so I went to the bathroom to wet it down. I swayed groggily down the hall and smiled when I saw a pile of beer in the kitchen. I always felt better around new people if I was drinking.

"Hey, you're up!" Riki said. "This is Angie and Mike."

I nodded and sat in a lawn chair.

"Who wants a beer?" Riki ducked into the kitchen, came back with a six-pack, and handed them around.

I grabbed one and cracked it like the old pro I was. It was still cold from the store.

Riki sat down, cracked their beer, and smiled. "This is a celebration for my new job."

"Great news!" I held up my can so they could tap it with theirs. "What is it?"

"I'll show you," Riki said, digging in their coat pocket.

I lit a cigarette and tried to guess what clue to a person's job could be tucked inside their pocket. Riki pulled out some tinfoil and unwrapped it carefully to expose an uneven dark brown ball.

"It's from Afghanistan. Pure hash," they said, eyes glinting. "My friend has a line on how to get it really cheap. If I sell enough of it, I can make a lot of money."

Mike and Angie broke into applause, like Riki had just given a graduation speech. I tried to look blank. I knew a lot of people in Calgary who had moved out to the Kootenays to grow weed, but when Riki had mentioned a job, I'd thought they would be working at a café or something, like me.

"Cool," was all I said.

I decided it was too late to do much about it. These were my new friends. I didn't know anyone else in the city except Sam, so I was just going to have to accept Riki's way of doing things.

We all drank another round, and then Riki started pinching small pieces off the brown ball and rolling them into tinier balls. The beer was starting to make me feel lighter when I heard someone strike a match in the kitchen to start up the gas stove. I went into the kitchen to see Riki leaning over the burner, interlacing two knives so the metal parts of the element held them into the fire. The flames were blue, except where the tips of the knives turned them orange.

"Grab a straw," Riki said to Angie, who pulled a bent but rinsed one out of a drawer.

The four of them went to work on the tiny balls of hash. Riki would press one between the two hot blades right after pulling them off the element. They passed the straw around and took turns holding the knives and sucking in the coil of smoke that came from the little ball. By the time one of them

It was dark out, but I wasn't scared.

offered it to me I felt like I was getting high enough just by hanging out in the kitchen. I told them I was going to get more beer and left the apartment.

It was dark out, but I wasn't scared. I remembered Riki saying that as long as I wasn't involved in anything, most people would leave me alone. It was a quarter to eleven, so the store was going to close soon. I skidded in and spotted a section for eight percent beer. That would do the trick! I grabbed a pack of T.N.T beer that was painted to look like a cylindrical wooden dynamite crate. Perfect.

When I got back to the top of the stairs I could hear a cacophony before I even opened the apartment door. There was a crashing, followed by an uproar of laughter. I caught a flash of Emily and Mike getting up off the floor and putting the white lawn chairs on their heads. Then they charged at each other like two elk in mating season.

I started laughing and couldn't stop. I cracked a beer and sucked half of it back. Then I hoisted a chair over my head, snorted to make everyone laugh, and charged at Mike. I knocked them down, catching them off guard, and the room cheered. Eventually, we all ended up on the floor, leaning our heads against the walls so we could see each other.

I shared the beer around and waited in the living room a couple of times while the others went to do more hot knives in the kitchen. When Angie and Mike left late into the night, I leaned on the walls like they were old friends to make it to the bathroom. When I tried to sit on the toilet I almost fell off, and then I crashed into bed next to Riki and passed out.

CHAPTER 11

The first sound I heard was the seagulls calling loudly.
Something was vibrating underneath me. I pulled the blanket
off and saw that I had slept in all my clothes. I clawed my
pager out from under me to see Sam's number on the little
screen. *Shit!* I should have invited Sam over last night.

Riki was still asleep. I leaned over to grab my cigarettes
from the floor next to the bed, lit one, inhaled a couple of
times, and tapped the ashes into a beer can next to the pack.
It had been a fun night, but I could feel myself spinning out.
I knew better than to just stand straight up. I finished my
cigarette and dropped it into the can, where it hissed at the
bottom. I braced myself and stood up slowly. The spinning
was worse higher up. I made it to the toilet and slumped onto
it to pee. I realized I was thirsty and leaned over the sink,
filling my hands from the tap again and again.

I made some coffee and noticed we were almost out. The
blackened knives were in the bottom of the sink. I checked

the time on my pager and realized I needed to leave for work. I put a cup of coffee next to Riki and took off up the Drive.

Outside, the sun was at its zenith. The sidewalk seemed steeper than usual and I felt the hill in my legs. I passed Grandview Park and walked through a waft of weed smoke from the usual semicircles of people hanging out there. My friends in Calgary would never have smoked weed out in the open like that. I never really liked weed anyway. I thought about the time I tried to smoke it alone when I was living with my grandma. I was sitting inside a steel rocket in a playground. I leaned back, lit a few small buds in the black bowl of my pipe, and inhaled deeply. As a floating feeling hit me, I heard a siren somewhere in the distance. Instantly, I was filled with dread. My thoughts twisted and I came to the firm conclusion that it was me they were after. I fled through the alleys back to my grandmother's house. Grandma wasn't home, so I scrambled with the lock on the front door. It wasn't until I was hiding in my room that the high started to wear off. After all that, I had barely smoked anything.

My heart was racing as I continued up the Drive.

My heart was racing as I continued up the Drive. I was going to arrive at work either just in time or a little late, so I picked up the pace. When the laundromat appeared, I slowed down and entered with something of a pleasant look on my face.

Sharon was alone at the counter, cashing out with a calculator. "Hey," they said, barely looking up. "I've got you working alone today. Do you think you're ready?"

"Sure."

"Cool. Someone just told me there's a mess in the bathroom. Do you mind cleaning it up before I leave? I haven't had a chance to do it."

I grabbed the broom and dustpan and headed into the bathroom. Before I clicked the light on I caught a whiff of a smell I couldn't quite place, like burned plastic. The fan whirred as I swept up a pile of curved and brownish pieces of glass on the floor. I made sure to check behind the toilet with the broom for more. There wasn't much glass in the pan, maybe the length of half a drinking straw if I'd glued it back together.

When I came back out Sharon handed me a paper bag for the pieces. "You good closing up by yourself? This is the alarm code." They pointed at a piece of paper with writing on it: *6666.* "Make sure you leave pretty fast after you enter it."

Sharon's boyfriend arrived and Sharon grabbed their hand. "Don't forget the code," Sharon called over their shoulder.

It seemed like it was going to be a slow day. It had started raining and the café was empty. First, I checked all the food bins to see what we were low on. I cut jalapenos, and then carefully washed my hands three times with soap. I kept forgetting that I had the oil on my hands, and my eyes were still burning from when I'd rubbed them after staring out the front window. The rain went on and on.

The banana peppers in the tray caught my eye. I took one out and cut off the smallest piece and placed it in my mouth. Fire! It was almost unbearable, like a snakebite or a burn on my wrist from the inside of the oven. I swallowed and the heat kept throbbing in my mouth. It was supposed to stop at some point, right? For the first time since I left the church, the word "faith" came into my mind.

My thoughts skipped around from one thing to another until I remembered Sam. I could call them to distract myself from the pain. I punched their number into the cordless phone next to the cash. Sam's mom picked up, and after a quick greeting, called Sam's name.

Sam picked up the phone. "Hello?"

"Hi, you paged me?" I said.

"Oh, yeah. We're coming up near you tonight. We're going to meet Ocean's sister and some other friends at Trout Lake after dark. We'll still be there when you get off work. I already talked to Riki and they said they'd come too."

"Sounds good."

"Riki will come walk with you when you get off work—"

"Wait, isn't it going to be raining?" I said, noticing that the burning in my mouth had stopped. Someone came in from the rain and walked up to the counter in front of me.

"Oy," they said, in sort of a rough greeting.

"I have to go, Sam."

"Okay, see you soon."

I faced my new customer. "Here to do laundry?"

"I could do it outside if I held it up." I thought I heard a cockney accent. "No, love. I did it yesterday."

"Okay, what can I get you?"

"I'll take a Molson Canadian." My mind flashed to the brewery near Kim's house. "Make it two," they said.

Behind them was a person with a perfectly groomed beard, holding a black garbage bag.

"Do you want those sorted?" I asked, as the first customer went and sat at a table.

"It's okay. It's only lights anyway."

"Cool." I ripped off half a ticket and handed it to them, keeping the other half to attach to the laundry bag.

"I'll be back early tomorrow."

"Sure," I said, noticing the person I had just given the two beers to had gotten back in line right behind them.

"The name's Mick," they said. "Have you ever heard Joe Cocker?" They were holding a portable CD player half out of their pocket with one hand and the headphones in the other.

"No."

"Joe sings like an angel. You have to hear it," they said, extending the earbuds towards me.

The thought of putting those earbuds into my ears, not to mention the close proximity to Mick that would be required for me to listen to a player they were was holding, grated on my nerves.

"I'm good," I said. "I have to do this right now." I held up the bag of laundry like a weapon and headed into the laundromat.

When I came back to the counter Mick was sitting at their table with their headphones in, peeling the label off their empty beer bottle and drinking the second one. When I was sure no one was watching, I ate some tortilla chips out of the bin. Then I washed my hands and topped up every bin. I roasted a tray of garlic the way I had been shown, with the cloves up. The savoury smell competed with the detergent from the other room. I pulled the hot tray out of the toaster oven, noting that all the garlic cloves were soft and lightly browned. I was about to start squeezing the garlic out when I caught Mick out the corner of my eye, headed back to the cash register. I checked the clock to see if I could use changing the load I was washing as an escape.

"I'll take another Molson," they said.

I looked at them and thought about intoxication laws, but Mick wasn't drunk enough to kick out. And it was getting close to closing time. One more was okay to sell.

Then they came out with, "'Do you know why I never drink Kokanee beer?"

I looked over at the lines of Kokanee bottles and frowned at the fact that Mick was still talking.

"It's because I took a shit on the Kokanee glacier. I just took my pants off and walked across it, shitting everywhere, like this." Mick squatted down to demonstrate.

Not sure what to say, I dropped Mick's change onto the counter forcefully. "Here you go."

They'd scooped it into their pocket instead of tipping me and inhaled like they were about to start into another story when Riki walked through the door. My heart jumped. They weren't soaking wet like I'd expected. I guessed the rain had finally stopped.

Riki beamed at me. "You off in less than an hour?"

"Yeah. Can I get you anything?"

"A beer?"

I almost grabbed a Kokanee, but I didn't want to get Mick going again. I passed Riki a Molson instead. While Riki sipped beer at one of the tables, I started my closing duties. To my relief, Mick slipped away while I was cleaning one of the washrooms.

Before I cashed out, I bought Riki's Molson plus six beers at my staff discount. I stuffed them into my backpack, turned off all the lights, grabbed my coat, and met Riki at the front. The code pad blipped as I pressed the 6 button four times and waited for the display to read *Armed*. The alarm started beeping rhythmically as we walked out, and I closed and locked the door as quickly as possible, fearing some sort of disaster.

CHAPTER 12

The rain had stopped and the sun had been able to almost dry the sidewalks. I realized Vancouver was a lot farther south than Calgary; back there, the sun would have still been up at this hour, reaching out for a long twilight.

Street lights lit our path as Riki and I walked to Trout Lake. I didn't hear the drums until my feet hit the grass of the park. The fastest way to the sound was straight across the soggy lawn. We arrived to find five or six people sitting in a circle on a wide T-shaped dock on the smallest thing I'd ever heard called a lake. Sam's laughter echoed across the field, and I felt how long it had been since I'd seen anyone I'd known for ten days.

"Hey, you two!" Sam called to us. "I feel like I haven't seen you in years!"

"Maybe you should come east more often," Riki joked.

"Maybe I will," Sam lobbed back. "This is Lisa, Ocean's sister, and Cara, Amy, and Lane."

The group opened their circle to let us in. I sat between Amy and Lisa, while Riki sat between Sam and Cara. For a second, I wished I'd gotten to sit next to Sam.

Two drums sat in the middle of the circle. Lisa was holding a guitar but seemed to have forgotten it was there. I opened my backpack and handed a beer to Riki across the circle. They winked while they twisted the cap off and went back to talking to Sam. I pulled one out for myself and drank about a third of it in one swig, hoping Ocean's sister was nicer than Ocean was. But pretty soon I forgot the two were related. Amy and Lisa were trying to figure out how to play an Ani DiFranco song, and I shyly showed them how to shape some of the chords. After that they could sing it with gusto, and between them they knew about eighty percent of the lyrics. Ocean started tapping away on one of the drums. The familiar song about both hands was welcome.

When the song ended I could hear what Lane and Cara were saying. They each had a drink in their hand, and their voices were louder than the drum had been.

"You wouldn't?" Lane said and laughed.

"That depends. What would you give me?" Cara asked.

"How about a cheeseburger?" Lane answered.

"Hmmm. Yep. I like cheeseburgers," Cara said.

Suddenly, Cara stripped naked. It was warm out, but not that warm. Far from Wreck Beach and the sun, I wondered what was worth being that bold. Before anyone could ask what was going on, Cara stepped off the dock and into Trout Lake, screaming as they hit the water.

"Fuck! You're covered in goose shit," Sam said when Cara climbed back out and shook themselves off like a dog.

Cara wiped their eyes and said, "I'll do it again—for another cheeseburger."

Lane was doubled over howling. "Three cheeseburgers if you do it again!" they bellowed.

Everyone erupted in hoots while Cara stood up, jumped back in, and then got out again.

Lane lifted Cara's hand up above both their heads and said, in a TV announcer's voice, "Three cheeseburgers, everyone!"

By now I had cracked my third beer and was raising it high. Riki picked up the other drum and started playing while Ocean was still thumping along and Lisa strummed away on the guitar. I glowed inside. I loved hearing music that I wasn't playing. These must be the people I was here to meet.

After a while, Riki got up and sat next to me and asked how I was doing.

"All right," I said. "Cara was smart to jump in naked," I whispered. "At least they had something dry to put on." Even back in their clothes Cara still looked cold, shivering with wet hair.

"Are they together?" I asked.
"Hard to tell. They could be exes, or friends, or part-time lovers," Riki answered.

"Yeah, that was so funny. They were building up to that bet for quite a while. Lane almost had to jump in too, but I guess the cheeseburger offer changed the negotiation."

Lane was rubbing Cara's shoulders playfully now in an attempt to keep them warm.

"Are they together?" I asked.

"Hard to tell. They could be exes, or friends, or part-time lovers," Riki answered.

I wondered if anyone could tell Riki and I were together. I mean, we lived together, but it wasn't like we'd been in each other's laps all night.

Lane dropped down beside us. "Hey, either of you want a cheeseburger?"

"I'm good," I said. "That might be the dirtiest water I've ever seen anyone jump into."

"Yeah. I love Cara. They're always up for anything. So, what's your story?"

I'd usually be off put by such a direct question, but their curiosity seemed genuine. "I moved here from Calgary. You?"

"I'm from Kamloops," Lane said. "We probably came here for the same reason. Slow towns, except for when you're running from trucks."

Riki jumped in. "This can be a slow town too sometimes. Maybe fewer trucks." They butted out their cigarette on the dock, rubbed off the dying ember, and then placed the butt into a pile they were saving to throw away at the end of the night.

"Where are you from?" Lane asked.

"California. Near Los Angeles," Riki said.

"I've never been there. I heard it doesn't rain," Lane said.

"Yeah, not really. I've been soaking wet ever since I got here." Riki smiled, and Lane smiled back.

I was looking at Lane, and then at their clothes. They were wearing a beautiful shirt with embroidered roses on it and crisp new Dickies work pants. I looked down at my clothes and wondered for the first time in my life if I was wearing the right thing. Maybe there was a way to dress when you were queer. I was glad the two of them were talking because I was getting a fuzzy head at the end of my third beer. I sucked back the last of the warm suds at the bottom and looked in my backpack. There was one left.

"Share?" I asked, pulling out the last beer.

"Sure," Riki said. They took a slug and then offered it to Lane.

Lane glanced at Riki and took a swig, wiping their mouth after. "I haven't seen you two around much," they said. "We're all going to the Lava Lounge tomorrow night to dance. You should come meet up with us."

"Sounds good. What time are you going?" Riki asked.

"With pre-drinking, probably eleven. It's down on Granville, near Davie."

"Yeah, I think I know it," Riki said.

"Great! See you both there."

With that, Lane stood up and went over to Sam, probably inviting them as well. Cara sat down next to us in the space Lane had vacated. Someone must have found a spare sweat-shirt for them because they weren't shivering anymore.

"You want some?" Cara pulled a small bottle of whiskey out of the front pocket of the sweatshirt. "It's Fireball. Tastes like cinnamon."

"Yeah." I was feeling less shy, and took what I thought was a large enough drink to look cool without choking. But the cinnamon hit the back of my throat and I almost lost it. I swallowed quickly and exhaled. "Whew!"

"Whoa," Cara said and tousled my hair.

Riki took a small sip and said, "So where are you from?"

"I'm from Prince Albert. Not like the piercing." Cara giggled. "Like that town up north in Saskatchewan." Their smile was wide.

"I'm from Alberta," I interjected.

"Well, you'll be a lot warmer here this winter," Cara said. "My first January I couldn't believe I could feel my legs the whole month."

Cara offered me the bottle again and I took a smaller sip. This time the cinnamon reminded me of the gum I would sometimes sneak into church. I smiled back.

"Are you two coming to the Lava Lounge tomorrow?" Cara asked.

"Yeah, I think so," Riki said.

"Cool. So how long have you been here?" Cara asked.

"I moved here when I was fifteen," Riki grunted.

"I've been here a bit over a week," I said.

"Oh, new person! Nice. I moved here a few years ago, when I was twenty. I dropped out of college in Saskatoon, hitchhiked west, and just kept going until I hit the water." Cara continued, "You'll like it here. There are so many queer people. I didn't meet any in Prince Albert, and here I can go weeks hanging out just with queer people."

"That sounds awesome," I said.

Riki looked off, mumbled something inaudible, and then went over to Sam.

"I work at this café on Commercial," Cara said, not missing a beat. "If you ever come by I can give you some free beer. It's my secret queer discount."

"Is it near Vicious Cycle? The laundromat? That's where I work."

"Yeah, it's a couple blocks away. Did you come from there tonight?"

I nodded.

"Well, you would have passed the café on the way here. It's on the same side of the street. I guess we're work neighbours. I'd come by there, but I have laundry at my apartment. So you'll have to visit me."

I watched Riki finish their beer across the circle from me and felt around in my bag before I remembered we were out. All the off-sales from bars were over by now. Besides, I'd forgotten my debit card at home and only had fifty cents left over from buying beer after work. I shifted a bit, wondering if I could get some more whiskey from Cara, but then I spotted the empty bottle in the middle of the circle.

Cara stood up and announced they were cold and going to head home, and Lane decided to go with them. Sam, Ocean, Amy, and Lisa decided to take a cab back downtown, so they

"I could sure use another drink," I said as we shuffled down the Drive.

walked with Riki and me back to Commercial and Broadway, where they could hail one.

Riki and I were alone again.

"I could sure use another drink," I said as we shuffled down the Drive.

"Do you have any money on you?" Riki said.

I shook my head. I noticed we were passing Cara's café, and then realized we were going to pass Vicious Cycle. I stopped outside.

"You going to grab some beer here?" Riki asked.

I could always pay it back next shift. The cooler shone like a beacon through the front window. I paused, and then nodded. I turned my key in the lock and opened the door. The beeping alarm made me jump, but then I remembered that I had the code. Riki and I slipped inside, and I pressed 6-6-6-6 on the pad. The beeping stopped.

The café was different at night. It smelled like the memory of meals more than food itself. Mostly, it smelled like an old mop. I pulled six beers out of the cooler and put them in my bag. We left the café the same way we'd come in, setting the alarm and locking the door.

Riki and I cracked two beers for our walk home. There was no one on the street now and talking was easy as we sipped, holding hands.

"I'm going to make so much money with my new job," Riki said, smiling. "We'll be able to keep boxes of beer at the house."

"And we can buy a whole closet of queer clothes. Like those Dickies at Army & Navy," I said.

"Sure. We can share those." Riki laughed.

We polished off two more beers before we hit the apartment building. Upstairs, we undressed as we cracked open our final beers. We turned off the light and fell into bed. We tried to kiss but ended up falling asleep in a mess of limbs.

CHAPTER 13

Riki and I woke up on opposite sides of the bed. I thought about lighting a cigarette, but the whirring sound in my ears warned me not to. Riki had most of the blankets wrapped around them, but their bare legs were sticking out. I smiled, thinking about Cara jumping into the water twice. I spotted half a beer next to the bed. I checked to see if any cockroaches had managed to climb into the bottle and then tilted it to my lips.

"Ewww," Riki said, waking up.

I gulped what tasted like a lukewarm cup of bread and grimaced. "What? I'm hungover."

"I get it, but let's at least go out for some Caesars?" Riki implored.

We walked up to Avanti's at First and Commercial. The restaurant had so few windows that it was a perfect place to hide from the sun. After my first Caesar, I was sure I could keep my food down, so I ordered eggs and toast. When our breakfasts came Riki shook their empty glass and ordered a second round.

"I want to play more music," I said, stirring my eggs around on my plate with my fork.

No answer. Riki was looking at their pager.

"Riki?"

They stiffened and said, "You should play at some open stages. I'll ask around about shows."

I was beginning to realize that Riki really wasn't much of a talker, unless they were drunk or high or in front of a crowd. A lot of the time, it seemed like Riki was someplace else. We could be right next to each other, walking, eating, or sleeping, and I would wonder if they even knew I was there. It felt more and more like we just happened to be together and not that we'd chosen it.

It felt more and more like we just happened to be together and not that we'd chosen it.

When we got home Emily called out to us from the kitchen. "The sink is clogged!"

"We better call Beetlejuice," I said.

"I saw them in the hall yesterday and they told me they'd be away for a few days," Emily said.

"Let's just leave it for now," Riki said, sounding irritated.

"Okay," Emily said. They walked out of the kitchen and into their room.

Riki and I decided to go back to bed. After the spinning part of the hangover came the exhaustion. Better to wait it out lying down. Riki immediately turned away from me and fell asleep. I didn't try to touch them. Staring at Riki's back, I thought about my agenda. Back in Calgary, I used to write down when I was going to see my friends or play shows. Now it was blank except for my work shifts. I fell asleep wondering how I was ever going to make a whole new life on this side of the mountains, and how long it was going to take.

When I woke up it was sunset. We'd slept through the whole day. That was a relief. With the direction my thoughts were going in, it was better to be asleep. The last time I'd let them reel out like that I'd ended up too close to the train tracks.

Riki stirred. "What time is it?"

"It's after nine," I said, peering at my pager.

"Oh. We should get up."

Riki used the bathroom while I went to look for some food in the kitchen. The dishes piled on the counter reminded me the sink was clogged. My guitar was leaning against the wall in the corner of the living room, and I thought briefly about picking it up. The last rays of sun, a golden yellow, were gleaming into the room. I closed my eyes and let them hit my face.

Riki came up behind me and wrapped an arm around my front. "You still want to go out?" they asked into my ear.

"Sure."

It was almost dark when we got downtown. We jumped off the bus at a pizza place and after a couple of dollar slices I was feeling better. I was so hungry I ignored the cockroach I saw crawl over the menu and didn't point it out to Riki. I had gotten so used to seeing them at the apartment that they didn't make me jump anymore.

We threw away our greasy paper plates and walked to Davie and Granville. When we got to Lava Lounge there were people outside shrieking with laughter. They were all strangers, so Riki and I decided to smoke before going in. We leaned against a wall, away from the crowd.

"Hey, you know that Sam and Ocean have been talking about having an open relationship?" Riki said. "You know, stay together but see other people?"

I looked at Riki's face. "No. Did Sam tell you that last night?"

"Yeah, when you were jamming with Ocean's sister. Anyway, they're moving in together, but Sam was saying they don't want to be exclusive—to keep them from being too closed off from the world."

I took a drag of my cigarette. I hadn't heard of anything like this before. In Calgary we just dated until someone cheated, and then we'd try to fix it or break up. My relationships had mostly been a string of back-and-forth cataclysms. It was cool to think about how we could be with other people without getting in so much trouble or losing each other. Maybe this idea I'd never heard of was the solution.

"Sounds cool. How does it work?" I asked.

"I guess people just try to be nice to each other," Riki said.

"Have you done it before?"

"Yeah. I mean, I usually keep things casual when I'm first seeing someone. Moving in with you was a real surprise." They smiled. "But yeah, when my last relationship ended I was hoping I could try out different arrangements. I don't think two people being just with each other forever makes any sense."

I thought about my parents and how my father used to assure me they'd never get divorced. I thought it was my dad's way of telling me that my mom and I would never get away from them. Yet even my parents finally got divorced.

"Well, maybe we could do it too?"

"I was hoping you'd say that!" Riki said, clapping me on the back and then squeezing my shoulder.

I already felt less lonely. I looked around at the other people smoking. I lived with Riki, but I could be with anyone. Thinking of the possibilities made me feel like I'd already had three beers.

"You want to go in now?" Riki asked with a grin.

"Yep, I do," I said, kissing them on the mouth.

The thudding house music hit me in the chest the moment I opened the door. Lights exploded everywhere as we walked towards the source of the thumping. The music dropped and the dancing figures slowed to halftime in anticipation. This was followed by silence and a huge rising synth sound. Everyone lifted their hands and jumped as the beat came back in. There were people everywhere dancing with their shirts off. Some of them were wearing sports bras. A couple were even standing on top of the speakers.

That's when I spotted Lane. They were dancing alone over in one corner. The lights hit them like they were the only person I was supposed to be looking at. I forgot Riki was beside me for a minute and just watched Lane dance, wishing I felt free enough to do that.

Riki grabbed my hand. "Hey, can you get us some beers?"

"Sure."

On the way to the bar I spotted Sam and Ocean making out against a wall. I got in the long line for a drink and felt a tap on my shoulder. When I spun around Cara grabbed me and kissed me right on the mouth. No one had ever kissed me out of the blue like that. Before I had time to decide how I felt about it, Cara pulled back and smiled at me.

"How are you?" they asked.

"Hungover," I replied.

I ordered two beers. Cara ordered six shots and paid for my drinks too. Time was moving differently since they'd kissed me. Quicker or slower, I couldn't tell.

Cara grabbed the shots and led the way over to Sam and Ocean. "Come on!" Cara yelled to them. They stopped whispering to each other and followed us to where Lane and Riki were dancing together. I gave Riki a beer, and Cara handed everyone a shot. "To us!" they shouted.

It was Jack Daniel's, which I used to put in my flask when I went out skateboarding at night in Calgary. The liquor achieved its purpose quickly, making my hangover a distant memory. I chased it with a slug of beer. In that moment, I felt like my life was really starting. All the talking in my head went quiet, the music filled my whole body, and that was it—the first time I ever danced, for real, even though it was more like jumping on a diving board. Everyone was dancing and smiling at each other. Cara kissed Ocean and Sam kept dancing. It was all so easy that I wondered why I'd never thought of letting go like this before.

Lane and Riki were yelling to each other while they danced, and then Riki went to the bathroom and Lane danced over to me.

"Hey, it's good to see you. You look really great!"

"I've never danced before." I blushed. "Just trying it out."

"Well, I like your energy. I can see people's energy, and yours is red."

"Thanks."

We danced, smiling at each other, for the rest of the song. I wondered if Lane smiled that way at everyone. It made me blush again, but I didn't worry because we were in a dark bar. Then Riki came back, downed their beer, and started dancing with us. It felt strange dancing with both Riki and Lane, but I knew we were all free to do whatever we wanted. Then Riki got closer to Lane and my good feelings took a dive. Why had Riki waited until we were about to meet up with Lane to bring up an open relationship? Did Riki like Lane? Riki hadn't said anything about what would happen if we both liked the same person. Maybe Riki and Lane had planned this last night. An easy way to get rid of me.

I panicked. I needed to go somewhere I could think. I saw a covered-up pool table on the far edge of the dance floor and dove towards it for refuge, rolling under it commando style.

From my position lying on my stomach I could only see feet churning on the cement floor. It wasn't as dirty under the table as I'd thought it might be. I put my head down on my arms, which were crossed in front of me, and tried to slow my thoughts down. What did I want? I wanted to be with Riki. We had just moved in together, and I didn't really know anyone else in the city. I thought Lane would be nice to hang out with. But what would that mean for Riki and me?

Suddenly, I felt a warm thud against my side. It was Riki. They'd rolled in after me.

"What's wrong?" they asked.

"I don't know how to do this open thing. Do you like Lane?"

"I don't know how to do this open thing. Do you like Lane?"

"Yeah, a bit. Do you?"

"I think so. Does that mean we have to have a threesome?" I asked.

"Nah, I'm not really into that. I've tried it and it's too much for me."

"Me neither. So, maybe just one of us should like Lane?" I said.

Riki seemed to think about it for a moment. "Yeah, maybe. Um, what if we tossed a coin?"

That seemed both strange and fair to me. "Sure," I said, digging in my pocket and handing Riki a quarter.

"Heads or tails?" Riki said, a huge grin on their face.

"Heads," I said as the coin flew up and hit the bottom of the table before landing between us. The caribou was facing up and seemed to be grinning at me.

"All right," Riki said. "You sure?"

"Totally."

Riki rolled out from under the table, but I stayed there a while. It was fair. I was just going to have to deal with it. Without Lane as a prospect, I was going to have to find someone else to be interested in.

I rolled out from under the table and went to the washroom. I liked these bars where whatever washroom I went to seemed to have people of all genders hanging out inside. I was starting to feel dizzy. The shot probably hadn't been a good idea. I leaned over a toilet to see if I had to throw up, but nothing happened. When I opened the stall door Cara was waiting outside of it. They grabbed me and kissed me again. I pushed them away, mumbling, "I feel sick." Cara gave me an injured look and left.

On the dance floor everyone seemed to be entwined. Since I wasn't interested in Cara, Sam, or Ocean, I counted myself out of whatever was going on. After that quick math I grabbed my sweatshirt from the coat check without saying goodbye.

I remembered Riki telling me that you could get beer after hours at the Chinese restaurant across the street. I got a table for one and ordered a "late tea." The server came back with a teapot full of light, yellow beer that looked just like green tea in my tiny cup. Genius.

I could see the doors of the bar from my seat at the restaurant. Twenty minutes later, Ocean, Sam, and Cara came out laughing and holding each other up. I decided I couldn't bear to see Lane and Riki leave together, so I paid for my "tea" and got a bus home.

CHAPTER 14

That night I woke up every hour on the hour. I hadn't been sleeping next to Riki for long, but it was now impossible for me to sleep without them. Every time I woke up my heart would start pounding and I'd be on the edge of tears. Why did sleeping alone make me feel like someone bad was coming to get me? It felt like the nights after my father left that I spent still waiting to hear them outside my room.

I gave up when the sun finally started to rise. I went to the kitchen and saw the mountain of dishes. Almost every dish in the house was in the pile. In a frenzy, I took them to the bathtub by the armload. I washed off all the crusted food, and then took them back to the kitchen to dry. Back in the bathroom, I sloshed all the chunks of food down the drain and then plugged and filled the tub. Sitting in the water with my arms curled around my knees, I couldn't make myself reach for the soap or put my head under. I turned the water off right before it was about to flow over the sides and sat there until it went cold. Then I stood up and let the water drain out. It was still draining ten minutes later.

Emily came out of their room and went to the kitchen. They let out a whistle. "Hey, you did the dishes. Right on. Did the landlord get back?"

"Nah, I did them in the bathtub," I said.

My pager went off with Sam's number. I remembered that Emily let Riki borrow their cellphone on weekends because it was free then, so I said, "Hey, Emily, can I borrow your phone for a second?"

"Sure." They handed over the little Nokia they always carried in their pocket.

I keyed in Sam's number and heard it ring with a little bit of crackle. "Hello?"

"Hi, you paged me?" I said.

"Oh, hi. I just wanted to see if you're okay. You disappeared last night."

"I'm okay. I'm at home. Riki hasn't come back yet, but they were with Lane, so I'm sure they're fine." My voice trembled. "Sam?"

"Yeah?"

"Is it always this hard? You know ... being open with people?"

"It can be really hard. But it's hard being with just one person too, right?"

I thought about it. So far, I'd been no good at being with one person. "Yeah," I said, resolved.

"Hey, what are you doing tomorrow?" Sam asked.

"I'm working."

"Too bad. There's a queer open stage at Cafe Deux Soleils. You could have played."

"Shit. I really want to play soon."

"It'll happen. Don't worry."

"Thanks for calling, Sam."

"No worries. I'll talk to you soon."

Emily was smoking on their bed and thumbing through a line of CDs.

"Thanks for letting me use your phone," I said, handing it back.

"No problem. Hey, where's Riki?"

"Out hooking up with someone else," I blurted, surprised at my honesty.

Emily looked up. "You're okay with that?" they said.

"We decided to have an open relationship."

"Oh, okay ..." They looked back down at the CDs.

I went to my room and shut the door. And then it hit me. That pure feeling of being lost. Hot tears started to stream down my face. I tried to cry quietly, face down into a pillow. I had a shift in a couple of hours. At least I had somewhere I needed to be. I set an alarm on my pager and fell asleep again.

When my pager went off, I went to the bathroom and washed my face. The bathtub still hadn't fully drained, but I didn't have time to worry about it. I grabbed my keys and my sweatshirt and took off up the Drive, walking as fast as I could. It made me feel better.

I had a friend back in Calgary who walked everywhere. Their Mormon parents had kicked them out when they were eighteen, but a year later they were back in Calgary, living in their parents' basement again. My friend didn't talk much about that year they spent in Montreal. One time we both stayed out too late for the buses, drinking at a bike courier bar downtown called the Castle, and I agreed to accompany them on one of their walking journeys. The neighbourhoods of the suburbs and the enormous fields of grass between them repeated themselves indefinitely. It took four hours to get to their parents' house, but I understood my friend more by the end of that walk. When life was unkind to us we could choose movement, the act of leaving a place to move to another. That way, we had somewhere to go when there was nowhere we felt welcome or safe.

When life was unkind to us we could choose movement, the act of leaving a place to move to another.

But Vancouver was not as sprawling as Calgary, and the laundromat was only a few blocks away. I focused just on getting there, not on how I was going to get through a shift with a broken brain. I tried not to think about the person whose name made me feel like I was deep under water.

When I walked into the café Sharon looked at me and then looked down as I approached. I often read people wrong and think they hate me. That's what I thought was happening with Sharon, so I tried to shake off the bad feeling. But Sharon stood up to block my way when I was about to go behind the counter to start working.

"It's hard for me to say this, but I have to let you go."

"Let's sit down," Sharon said and guided me to a table, where they sat down and pulled a black rectangular book out of their purse. "It's hard for me to say this, but I have to let you go."

My lips moved a bit, but I had nothing to say in return. It didn't occur to me to ask why.

"We can't have you working here anymore," Sharon said and opened the chequebook.

They wrote out a number that started with a three, filled out the rest of the cheque, and scrawled their signature at the bottom. That was when I spotted a camera perched high above us on one of the shelves, pointed at the door. Now I knew why.

"Thanks," I said, knowing I was deep in the wrong.

I wanted to explain that I was going to pay for the beer as soon as I got on shift today, that I would have paid last night if the till wasn't closed, and that I had never stolen anything in my life, but I'd already gotten up and walked out before my thoughts finished. And then I was standing on Commercial Drive, jobless again.

I drifted back towards the apartment, not like I was under water but more like I was a tumbleweed. I tried to embrace my new free hours by buying two six-packs of beer. On the journey home I carried a bag in each hand, letting them weigh me down like I was a balloon float in a parade.

The three flights of stairs up to our apartment were no longer a challenge. My legs had become used to them.

Emily came into the kitchen as I was loading beer into the fridge and asked, "Have you seen Riki?"

"No, not yet." A lump rose in my throat. "You want a beer?"

"Sure."

I ripped one off the plastic ring and handed it to them. Emily walked into the living room and I followed, cracking my own beer. I was starting to feel pretty hollow after so many days of drinking in a row. Three days into a bender I always felt like I was chasing down the idea of remembering myself.

"How are you doing?" Emily asked.

I let some tears roll down my cheeks. I was silent long enough that Emily knew they had to carry the conversation.

"You and Riki having trouble?"

"I don't know. We opened our relationship last night and I'm trying to learn how to do it." I sniffed. "Then I went to my job today and they said they don't need me anymore."

Those were two unsolvable problems. Emily's eyes grew warm. They changed the subject. "The toilet is clogged."

"Ugh. Did you try a plunger?"

"I borrowed the neighbour's, but it didn't do anything."

I heard the lock in the door turn and wiped my face. I didn't want Riki to see me upset.

Riki walked into the living room and said "Hey" while looking at both of us. They went into the kitchen and grabbed a beer.

"Toilet's clogged!" Emily yelled after them.

I heard Riki sigh, and then nothing. It was like they were counting down to talking to us. Emily made a face at me and I almost laughed. Then Riki came back in and settled into one of the white lawn chairs. They were wearing the same clothes from last night, yet they looked different.

"I thought you had work?" Riki said, crossing one leg over the other. "I went by and Keith said you weren't working there anymore. They looked super sad about it."

"Sharon told me they didn't need me anymore." I looked down.

"Shit! Well, lots of jobs in this city," Riki said.

"Yeah." I looked at my beer and let that be my entire answer.

"That sucks anyway," Riki said, finally looking into my eyes for longer than a few seconds.

My chest felt a bit warmer, and I mumbled, "Yeah."

"What are we going to do about the toilet?" Emily said, bringing me back into the room.

"Well, we can pee in there as long as we don't fill it all the way up," Riki said.

"I hope the landlord gets home soon," Emily said.

"I think it's the day after tomorrow," Riki said. "Besides, it may not be only our suite. I bet there are problems below us too, if we have them."

Emily shrugged and got up, finishing their beer. "Yeah, we'll figure it out." They went to the bathroom without flushing and then into their room.

The sun was almost down now and the street lights were on. The Gap baby was lit up and grimacing over Hastings

Street. Riki and I quietly slugged on our beers, and then Riki got us two more. It felt like years had passed since I'd stepped off the bus from the airport and met Riki.

"Sorry I was gone so long without paging you," Riki said. "By the time I woke up I figured you were at work."

"That's okay. You should do what you want," I mumbled.

I rolled the word "want" around in my mind for a while, waiting to see if thinking about it would let me know what I wanted. I *wanted* to get away from Calgary. I *wanted* to be around more queer people. I *wanted* to be with Riki. Yet I didn't know how to maintain all these new things. When I was growing up, I'd never pictured my adult life. I knew queer people didn't do things like other people, but I'd never quite been able to figure out how to behave. I used to think I probably wouldn't survive that long, anyway. I didn't want Riki to catch wind of how lost I was. It was all just a dance I was going to have to learn.

"I'm glad you're home," I said, touching their arm on my way to the bathroom.

I knew now that Riki was no longer on my team. I'd always had to stay one step ahead. Of my parents, who would have sent me to conversion therapy. Of the people at my school and on the street who wanted to hurt me for being queer. I had to spot aggression before it spotted me and decide if I should disappear or risk a confrontation. In Vancouver, I'd been able to put a lot of that knowledge away. Few people here seemed to want to hurt me for being queer. Instead, it seemed as if the queers were hurting each other.

CHAPTER 15

Riki and I ended up making out most of the next morning
because that's something I can do more easily when I don't feel
like myself and don't feel like talking. After, I was lying on the
bed, staring out the window at the power lines, when I heard
Riki swearing in the bathroom. They slammed the door open
and stomped into the kitchen. Then I heard them hurry back
into the bathroom, where they spent a few minutes before
rushing through our room with a white grocery bag held out
in front of them. A foul smell filled the room. They dropped
the bag out of our third-storey window into the Dumpster
below, where it landed with a thud.

Riki turned to me and said, "Toilet's still clogged."

I started laughing and couldn't stop. It ramped up to a howl
while I held my stomach under the covers. Riki couldn't help
but join me in a fit of manic giggles.

Maybe the point was that there was no point. We were
just going to do whatever we wanted all the time.

Riki crawled back into bed, wrapped an arm around me from behind, and breathed on the back of my neck. Such a short time had passed, and yet everything felt different.

"Riki?"

"Yeah?"

"Do we just keep going on like this?"

"I always have," they whispered.

I felt sleep coming over me and we both passed out again.

The creak of the front door opening woke me up. I heard a lot of sloshing sounds, and then the toilet flushing over and over.

"Beetlejuice is back," I whispered to myself, smiling.

I wasn't going to have to shit into a grocery bag after all. I drifted back to sleep, completely relaxed.

When I woke up I tested the kitchen sink and the bathtub before flushing the toilet. Beetlejuice must have dumped drain cleaner in every orifice of the apartment. The water gargled down through our building's pipes and into the city drains as fast as I could pour it.

I would run out of money after next month's rent, so I needed to get a new job. Riki knocked on the bathroom door and I realized I'd been giving myself this real talk at the sink with the water running. I quickly unlocked the door and exclaimed, "It's working!"

I was sitting on our bed when Riki came back from the bathroom. "Sam wants to know if we want to go to Cafe Deux Soleils tonight for that open mic," they said. "It's all queer."

"Sounds good. I could bring my guitar."

"You want me to play with you?"

I nodded and went to the living room. I strummed my guitar, and the sound pulled me together, as if I were made up of balls of mercury that were suddenly able to find each other. It had been almost week since I'd sung anything. I lifted my voice out of hiding with a song I'd written.

This was why I was here. If there were people who could just listen to me sing without caring about how I looked, I would have a chance in Vancouver. This was what I really wanted to do.

Riki started accompanying me on the hand drum, and it sounded really good. We finished the first song, and I led us right into the next. Riki moved with the rhythm without overpowering it. Maybe we were together again.

I lifted my voice out of hiding with a song I'd written.

When we arrived at the café there was a crowd of people smoking outside and complaining about the new smoking law.

"I'll sign us up on the list," Riki said.

I saw Cara at the bar and smiled. I still only knew about fifteen people by name in the whole city.

I walked up to them, grinning, and said, "Queer discount?" in the boldest voice I could muster.

"You had your chance," Cara said in a neutral tone.

That caught me off guard. So the queer discount wasn't free.

"Okay, well, I'll take a pint of whatever that is," I said, pointing to a tap with a big rubber gumboot on it.

Cara put my beer down in front of me with a gentler look on their face. "Here you go. Let me know if you ever change your mind."

I answered by sucking a small amount of foam off my beer, and then smiling at Cara before turning around.

"Hey y'all. This is it. Cat Call, the all-queer open stage. Our first performer is the handsome Drake!"

The chorus of "The Real Slim Shady" started pumping through the speakers. I felt cornered, but beer wasn't allowed outside, so I stood as still as I could as the crowd went wild for Drake again. I peered at the performer's bobbing crotch and thought about the hard life of the teddy bear that was crammed in there. I leaned against the bar and focused on keeping my face as neutral as possible.

Finally, the teddy bear emerged for all to see and the host announced, "Okay, next up is Frond. Let's get really quiet because they've brought us the gift of poetry."

After everyone settled down a figure in a dark green caftan came onstage. "Hello," Frond whispered into the microphone, their voice husky. They tried to adjust it to be shorter, with little success.

The host came back onstage, lowered the mic, and left again.

"I've had a really hard week. I wanted to have a poem prepared for tonight, but I couldn't sleep last night and I just couldn't put anything down. But I realized that poetry is all around us. I mean ..." They paused. "... Maybe poetry is all that we are."

They pulled the caftan off over their head and dropped it on the stage. They weren't wearing a thing underneath. I blushed and looked at the floor.

Frond's voice was shaking a bit as they continued. "My body is the only poetry I have today. I used to hate my body, but I don't want to anymore. I won't blame myself anymore. This is me. Take it or leave it. If you're going to leave it, say it to my face. I am poetry!"

With that, they stepped back from the microphone to thunderous applause. People started whistling like we were at a hockey game. Frond picked up the caftan and walked slowly offstage, smiling and waving.

I felt sick to my stomach. My ability to handle unexpected sex and nudity hadn't improved in the past few weeks. I finished my beer and went to get another one. Suddenly, my name and Riki's were called out from the stage. I bolted out of the bar line, picked up my guitar case, and unzipped it next to the stage. Riki had their drum in hand and was busy finding a chair to sit on. The short delay of us setting up had caused people to turn their heads away from the stage; the crowd was now talking loudly and laughing.

I walked to the mic and tilted it up to my mouth. For the first time since I'd been in Vancouver I felt like I knew where I was. I had played enough shows in bars in Calgary to know which of my songs would get people's attention. I picked one about an adventure with my friends when we broke into an outdoor swimming pool at night and a police helicopter chased us out. I began the guitar intro and Riki started hitting their drum. The talking quieted down and people turned towards us. I breathed deeply and started singing. The song was fast and funny, and I put everything I had into singing the words clearly into the microphone. In the middle of the song I signalled for Riki to take a drum solo, which got everyone cheering. And then I got everyone to sing along to the chorus at the end. When Riki and I left the stage, everyone's eyes looked different, like they all knew me and liked me.

I went outside to smoke and found Riki was already there, leaning against a wall with a circle of people around them.

"That was awesome!" Lane said, patting my back.

I smiled and sat on the curb a bit away from everyone and listened to the café door opening and closing over and over. I felt the back of my head and it was sweaty. I had been nervous, but now that it was over I felt like I was flying. I kept smiling.

Just then, Frond plopped down next to me. "Hey, nice song! Are you and Riki dating?"

"Yeah. I mean, we're open," I said, unsure how I was supposed to talk about our relationship in public. The declaration turned my sweat cold, and my stage high started to dissipate.

"Lane and I have been trying the open relationship thing too," Frond said. "Do you have a hard time when Riki stays out all night?"

"It's ..." I hesitated, taken aback by Frond's sudden intrusion. "New ..."

"Like last night, when Riki was out with Lane?" Frond pushed.

"Yeah." I felt lower with every second I spent near this person.

"Do you know where I was that night?"

"Where?" I felt sick asking.

"I was sleeping on my own couch! Can you believe it? The door to our bedroom was locked. Lane and Riki wouldn't open it, even though I banged on the door and screamed for an hour. There's a bathroom in there, so neither of those rats had any reason to come out."

I started to cower at the image of Lane and Riki in bed. I didn't want to picture them together.

"You want to know the worst thing?" Frond said, and then steamrolled on before I could respond. "They were under my quilt. My quilt! The one my grandmother made me."

I didn't feel like Frond was really talking to me anymore. I could have been anyone. They just wanted to vent. I wanted to change the subject so I could get the picture of Riki and Lane entwined under some grandma-blanket out of my head.

I didn't know what to say, so I said, "Good performance. Way to get naked!"

Oh, fuck. Well, that was it. The very worst thing I could say.

But Frond continued as if I hadn't said anything at all. "Come to think of it ... where are they?"

And that's when I saw a bit of Riki's pant leg sticking out of a hedge in the lot next to the café. I could see two pairs of shoes and four legs.

Frond's eyes followed mine. Their nostrils enlarged astronomically and they leapt up. "That's it, Lane, you asshole! I'm done!"

Frond went over and started swinging their arms at Lane and Riki like a kid slap-fighting. The slaps didn't look very hard, but Lane took off around the corner and Frond followed them. After a moment I heard a screech.

Riki stood alone, shoulders slumped and hands in their pockets, looking a bit stunned. I shrugged at them and they shuffled towards me. When they got close enough they tilted their head at me and tried a winning smile. It almost worked.

"I think Frond might be crazy," Riki said.

I wasn't going to slap anyone, but my ears were on fire with rage. I felt like throwing up. "I don't understand this, Riki," I said in a hushed tone. "The way you two disappeared was really messed up for Frond. It made me feel really bad, too. Yeah, it's messed up to go slapping at people, so maybe we should make sure we don't go to a place where either of us ever feels like doing it. I mean, maybe we should talk about how we're going to do this open relationship thing. Do people have different rules or anything?"

"We don't need all that. We can just play it by ear. You said you were cool with it last night," Riki said.

"Riki, last night has turned into today. Every day, we seem to be in a new situation where I'm surrounded by people and supposed to act like I don't care that you're off somewhere making out with someone else. And judging by the way Frond acted, it doesn't seem like Lane is communicating either. Maybe you could warn me if I'm going to have to see you making out with other people at an event we came to together? Isn't there some way we can do what we want without hurting each other? You seem to know so much about it. Tell me how."

"Rules are for straight people." Riki sniffed and looked down.

"So you're going to do whatever you want, no matter how I feel?" My eyes were wide with surprise.

"Yeah, pretty much. If you can't handle it, maybe you should go back to Calgary."

Those last words might as well have been a slap.

"You know what?" I seethed. "We're done talking." I walked inside to get another beer and Riki didn't come after me.

I was drinking my beer and feeling my pulse return to normal when someone tapped me on the shoulder.

I heard the words, "Hey, I'm Sam's friend," and then almost jumped back because of how astonishingly attractive the person's face was. "Sam said you were looking for a job? I manage a kitchen downtown and we're looking for some prep cooks."

I had the uncool urge to say, "Take me to the job. I will follow you anywhere!" but I managed to rein myself in.

"What does a prep cook do?" I asked.

"You cut things and stock up bins. Work the cold bar of the kitchen when customers order things. Sometimes do the dishes if the dishwasher isn't in yet or it gets busy."

"I'd love to," I said, feeling some relief.

"By the way, I really liked your song," they said.

"Thanks." I put my hands in my pockets and prayed not to blush.

"Have you been writing them for long?"

"Since I was twelve," I mumbled.

"Well, I'm glad I got to hear you play. Do you have a phone number so I can let you know when I have your training shifts worked out?"

"Sure," I said and scribbled my pager number and my name on the back of a flyer.

"Great. When are you free to work?"

"Anytime."

We held each other's eyes a little too long, and then both looked away.

"Okay, I'll call you soon."

They were turning to leave before I suddenly remembered to say, "Hey, wait! What's your name?"

"It's Hana."

The door of Cafe Deux Soleils swung closed, and I blushed from my ears to my neck.

CHAPTER 16

I made my way home by myself. I was at the height of the upswing of drinking, dangling on the precipice. I'd grown up trying to predict how people were going to behave. If Riki didn't hook up with Lane, it would be someone else. Or they'd find another way to show me they didn't give a shit. What about all the money Riki had gotten out of me? Had they ever even liked me? And where was I going to live now?

My thoughts spiralled into a darkness that spread until it filled everything in front of me. I saw a pay phone and was dialling before I realized what I was doing.

"Riki. Hey," I whispered after the voice mail greeting. "Where are you? We have to figure all this stuff out. Page me and let me know when you're going to come home."

I hung up the phone and started to sway, feeling blood flooding into my ears. I put another quarter in the phone and dialled Riki's number again.

My thoughts spiralled into a darkness that spread until it filled everything in front of me.

"You know what? I'm getting sick of this, Riki. You're being such an asshole. Come home right now and tell me you're leaving to my face." I felt guilty immediately after the words left my mouth. "I mean ..."

I hung up and walked away from the phone before I could pick it up again.

Before I got anywhere close to the apartment door I could hear loud noises. I knew it couldn't be Riki, so I welcomed the sound of anything other than my own dark thoughts. When I opened the door, there was silence, yet all the lights were on. I closed the door behind me, looking around for the source of the noise.

Suddenly, Mike, Angie, and Emily jumped out at me, screaming. I broke out in a huge grin. We all laughed and Emily handed me a beer. I put my guitar case down in the living room and sat in one of the white lawn chairs.

"What's up?" I said.

"We're just hanging out," Angie said. "Where's Riki?"

Seeing my face fall, Emily looked concerned, and then blurted, "Who cares?"

It was sweet of them to spare me having to explain. This was only the second time I'd hung out with Mike and Angie, but tonight they felt like my oldest friends.

"Can I play your guitar?" Angie asked.

"Sure." I unzipped the case and handed it to them.

They whistled, turning the guitar around before cradling it in their arms. "Nice!"

Mike looked like they'd just remembered something and yelled, "Monster truck rally!"

Angie smiled and started strumming some chords. "Okay," they said, and began to sing in a clear voice:

"Monster truck rally. Monster, monster truck rally.

Hey you, with the smelly breath and the hairy chest,

I saw you light an unfiltered Camel cigarette.

You're gonna take me to the ...

Monster truck rally. Monster, monster truck rally."

We made up more verses as we went along. They didn't have to make any sense. We all just sang along and swayed. Mike stomped his feet and I flicked my beer can in time.

We had repeated the chorus five or six times when the room abruptly went dark. Through the window I could see the power was out all the way to downtown. The Gap baby was enshrouded by the night. It was the visual equivalent of complete silence.

Then Mike started hooting, "Anarchy! Let's go outside in case there are riots!"

"Anarchy!" Angie echoed, bumping my guitar as they put it down.

We worked ourselves into a frenzy, gathering the necessary supplies of cigarettes and beer for the inevitable orgy of social breakdown. But when we got to the bottom of the stairs, we saw that the streets were hushed and still.

"No riots, Mike," Angie said. "I guess we're just going to have to walk you to your bus."

"I hate living in Ladner!" Mike wailed.

"Where's Ladner?" I asked.

"You'll find out if you ever take the bus to the ferry. It's a flat piece of land near the water," Angie explained.

We turned and saw that the houses on the mountains still had power. "Of course they have power in North Van!" Mike said.

Our effervescent mood evaporated as we walked with Mike. When his bus pulled up we all embraced in a group hug.

"I better go, too," Angie said. "But I'll walk you two home."

When we got back to the apartment building Emily barked a quick goodbye to Angie and started up the stairs.

"Hey," Angie said, "I love Riki, but I know how they can be. Here's my number if you ever need anything. You can crash on my couch for a while if things aren't going well over here."

"Thanks." I took a crumpled piece of paper out of Angie's hand as a lump started to block my throat.

I waited until Angie was halfway down the block and then yelled, "Anarchy!" I could hear them hooting down the street as they walked away.

I lay down because there was nothing else to do in the pitch black.

When I got upstairs, Emily was in their room and all the beer was gone. I lay down because there was nothing else to do in the pitch black. My pager was dark and silent. I lit a cigarette, but instead of the familiar flavour of tobacco, a sickly burning filled my throat. Coughing, I looked at the cigarette and saw that there was no glowing ember. I knew then that I'd lit it backwards.

CHAPTER 17

I woke up to my pager buzzing. I looked hopefully for Riki's number, but it was a voice mail. The power must have come back on during the night because all the lights were on. I walked around the apartment flicking them off and didn't hear any stirring in Emily's room. I made some coffee and then decided to walk to the pay phone outside Nick's Spaghetti House with my mug to check my messages.

"Hey, it's Hana. I know it's pretty soon to be calling, but someone quit today. If you can make it in this afternoon for training that would be great."

I dialled the number Hana gave me. "Hey, is this Hana?" I asked when a voice answered.

"Yeah, it is. Can you come in today?"

"Sure."

"The restaurant is down on Davie and Seymour. It's called DV8. You'd be on from three to eleven. Does that work?"

"Yeah, for sure."

"Okay. Wear comfortable shoes you don't mind getting food on."

I looked down at my one pair of shoes and shrugged. "Okay, see you soon." My hangover had disappeared.

I decided that if I was going to work late downtown, it was time to get my own bike, so I headed towards a pawn shop on Hastings instead of jumping on a bus. I bought a chrome BMX, mainly because the tires were full and I needed to ride it right away. When I got to Seymour Street it was like a different world from Hastings Street and East Vancouver. Everyone I passed was wearing office clothes and trying not to look at each other. I saw the DV8 sign and locked my bike to a post.

I opened the door to the sound of Thom Yorke singing. The restaurant smelled like old dishes with a hint of bottle-recycling plant.

A voice from the back shouted, "The kitchen's to the right."

Peering into the darkness, I saw a person at a table with piles of paper and a calculator in front of them. "I'm Jack, the owner," they said.

Hana came out to greet me and guided me to the back.

"This is Captain," Hana said, "the main cook here. I'm the kitchen manager."

"Ahoy-hoy," Captain said, offering me a high-five, which I accepted with a resounding clap.

"You're pretty strong for someone your size," Captain observed.

"I'll show you all the stuff on the cold line, and Captain will train you on the hot line as soon as orders start coming in," Hana said. "We have a couple of hours to prep before the restaurant opens."

"Great!"

"Here's your apron. You should also hang a towel through it like the Captain here to wipe your hands."

Captain had picked up a knife and started sharpening it with a goofy smile. Any other person, under any other circumstance, would have looked ominous.

Hana set to work showing me the cold bar and how to restock each container. After that they talked about what kinds of orders would come in, and how I would have to garnish burgers and add salads to hot plates as they came off the hot line.

I observed as closely as I could. I decided that I was going to have to learn how to look Hana in the face without blushing if I was actually going to learn anything. Besides, Hana seemed totally comfortable and self-assured.

Hana showed me how to sharpen my knife, which turned out to be an indispensable skill. The sharper my knife, the less resistance I encountered slicing things, so I sharpened it every chance I got. I also liked the repetitiveness of stocking each bin in solitude. This job felt like something I could do for a long time.

The restaurant finally opened and orders started to come in. Hana kept me on the cold line with them and taught me how to roll sushi and turn tortillas into wraps. I put lettuce and tomatoes on burgers and learned how to read the tiny paper chits to make sure I wasn't putting anything on the plate people didn't want, as well as adding any extras they requested. There was something exacting about fulfilling a food order that reminded me of playing music. Unless everything was right, it was wrong.

My pager buzzed under my apron and I asked Hana if I could take a break. When I called the number, Ocean picked up, but they handed the phone to Sam right away.

"Hey, you at your new job?"

"Yeah, I'm cooking at DV8."

"That was fast! Hana told me about the job, but I thought you'd have a few days before you started."

"Thanks for letting Hana know that I needed a job!"

"I'm so glad it worked out! Isn't Hana great?"

Could Sam already sense my attraction to Hana, or were they just being a supportive friend? "Maybe that night at the open stage was lucky after all," I said sardonically.

"Maybe that night at the open stage was lucky after all," I said sardonically.

"Yeah, I heard that Frond was talking at you, and then Lane and Frond had a huge fight. I'm sorry you were put in the middle of it. Anyway! You got a new job and that's great."

I did feel pretty happy that I wasn't unemployed anymore.

"Hey, we're going to a party tonight at my friend's house," Sam said. "Do you want to come?"

"Okay." I scratched down the directions Sam gave me on some scrap paper I found by the phone. "Hey, have you heard from Riki?" I asked, dropping my voice lower.

"They haven't been home?"

"Not unless they're there now." I sighed.

"Wow. That sucks. I'm sorry. I'll tell Riki to page you if I hear from them."

"Thanks, Sam."

I hung up the phone and held onto it for a moment longer instead of letting go. I wasn't sure if it was sadness or rage sweeping over me. It seemed like Riki was going to be unavailable for the breakup part of our relationship, too.

I went back to the kitchen and washed my hands. Captain was making a pasta sauce, and there was something bubbling in one of the deep fryer baskets. Captain started telling me about how they made orders on the hot line and I listened intently trying to push Riki out of my thoughts.

After a while, Hana came back into the kitchen and said, "Order in!"

Captain took the white chit and placed it behind two others where they hung over the range, and I made my way to the cold bar to finish off the plates.

Over the next few hours, five or six servers showed up. Unlike the kitchen staff, they were bubbly, dressed up in nice clothes, and found ways to mention they were actors. While kitchen workers had a tendency to swear and mumble, a lot of the servers/actors over-enunciated. I could tell they thought they were better than us, but they needed us to keep plating the food. If we didn't do it right, they wouldn't make their tips. So they made small talk over the hot plate and tried to keep things friendly.

I fell into the rhythm of the cold line and did some loads of dishes whenever I had a break from prepping or cooking. By the time Hana tapped me on the shoulder to let me know my shift was over, my sleeves were soaked with water and my apron had streaks of food all over it from where I'd wiped my knife and hands.

"You did great!" Hana said warmly. "Come back the day after tomorrow? Same time?"

"Sure."

"Great. By then I can add you to the schedule for next week and you'll know your hours."

"Thanks."

I threw my apron and towel into the laundry and walked out the back door. My shoes were covered in bits of food and I could smell the deep fryer on me. It wasn't a cold night, but the air bit through the parts of my clothes that had gotten soaked under my uniform.

Sam's directions were crumpled in my pocket, but I could remember the street names now. I stood up on my pedals and the wind started to dry my clothes as my bike built momentum. It was dark and I couldn't see the mountains. Vancouver could have been any other city. The oxygen-filled night air fuelled me, and I felt like I was flying towards something. I pumped my legs up and down. Nothing could stand in my way as long as I kept pushing myself forward.

Nothing could stand in my way as long as I kept pushing myself forward.

CHAPTER 18

I could hear the party from outside on the street, and there were bikes everywhere. The music was thumping, competing with the screeches of laughter coming from the backyard. I walked up to the gate expecting to see strangers, but instead I saw Riki, surrounded by people. Riki was so Riki in that moment, laughing and smoking like everything was perfect. I knew they wouldn't be able to come up with more than a couple of words for me. Riki stopped talking suddenly when they spotted me but regained their cool in a millisecond.

"Hey!" they said brightly and sauntered over.

The affection in their voice surprised me. I started to shake and didn't say anything.

"Hold this," they said, handing me their beer. They dug around in the pocket of their cargo shorts and produced a half-full mickey of vodka. "Here," Riki said as they handed it to me. "You're going to need this to be at this party." They snickered conspiratorially and started swaying. "An hour ago, Lisa passed out in the bathroom with the door locked and a bunch of people started peeing in the double kitchen sink two at a time. So nasty!"

I chuckled in spite of myself and slugged some of the vodka. "What are we going to do, Riki?" I asked.

"I don't know," Riki said.

The lost look on their face made me feel like they were telling the truth. Neither of us knew what we were doing.

"Do you still want to be with me?" I asked.

There was a long pause. "I really like you," Riki said slowly, touching my shoulder. Then they looked up at someone coming out of the basement door.

I followed their eyes to Lane. I took another slug off the bottle. Vodka is supposedly tasteless, but right then it tasted like something had gone off. I could feel myself shrinking, floating an inch above the pavement, and my ears were ringing. I wondered what the sound was, and then hit me. It was rage.

"You know what? Don't worry about it, Riki. I'm over it," I said through gritted teeth.

Lane moved over to us quickly. It seemed like they didn't want Riki and me to talk alone for even one more second. I sighed and suppressed an urge to scream at them as I brushed past and into the house. Riki couldn't leave me if I left them first.

Sam spotted me and screamed, "Yes! I'm so glad to see you. How's your new job?"

I still had Riki's bottle in my hand. "I really like it! Hana's so great! Thanks again for telling them about me!" I shouted my news over the music, hoping it would somehow get back to Riki.

Sam's good mood was my flotation device. With each new person I met I slugged on the bottle and felt the small thrill of being a little further away from myself. Yet the sadness was always just below my feet, threatening to pull me under.

With each new person I met I slugged on the bottle and felt the small thrill of being a little further away from myself.

Eventually, the bottle was empty. I searched through the blurriness taking over my vision and spotted Cara. I strutted over and said, "Is my chance over?"

Cara responded by pulling me onto a chair and kissing me. I held my breath, opened my mouth, and tried to kiss like I meant it instead of like a robot. I needed to stay ahead of the sadness and anger that was building into a tidal wave. I became nothing more than a body that responded to another body. As long as I kept moving with the swells, I could keep my head above water.

Then I felt a hand go up my shirt. I froze. The hand kept moving and my deepest instincts took over. I screamed, "Get the fuck off me!" and pulled myself out from under Cara with a preternatural burst of strength.

The music was too loud for anyone else to hear my outburst. Cara alone was looking at me, their eyes like a wounded animal's.

"I'm sorry," I said. "I forgot to tell you I don't like that."

That's when I knew I was going to throw up. I wobbled to the bathroom and made it to the toilet just in time. Convulsive heaving took over and I thought it would never end, until it did. I wiped my face and drank water from the bathroom tap. Beer was always good after I threw up, and in my experience, it always lived in the refrigerator at a party. I staggered into the kitchen, took a beer, and sat on the counter, surveying the room from my new perch.

Then I spotted Lane and Riki on the far side of the room, their limbs entangled as they kissed each other like they were the only ones at the party. My stomach subdivided over and over until it felt like it was made of dust. I watched myself walk over to the couch. I was nothing now. Nothing mattered except putting out that fire. My face must have been blank. I stood over Riki and Lane and unceremoniously dumped the rest of my beer over their heads.

"That's not cool!" someone yelled.

"You are so fucked up!" Riki screamed and stood up, soaked in beer.

I wondered who they were yelling at and looked behind me. Then I felt the eyes of everyone in the room on me.

"What the fuck is their problem?" I heard someone say.

I stumbled out of the house and back to my bike. After a block of wobbling forward, I felt the ground come up to meet my head. A burning sensation shot down my side. I wondered why I wasn't moving anymore and realized that I was still on my bike, but I had tipped over sideways. The front tire was spinning silently. I got up and slowly limped up Prior Street, the BMX and me holding each other up. My pager kept buzzing, but I didn't look at it.

I finally turned on Woodland Drive. I locked my bike in front of my building and crawled up the stairs. I could feel the road rash burning on my knee where it touched the carpet. Years later, the stairs ran out. I managed to get into the apartment after several attempts at unlocking the door. I didn't bother to turn on the lights.

I walked into my room, saying hello to the window like an old friend. The pain from my fall was starting to throb with my pulse. In the blue light of the moon, I saw bloody scrapes on my arm that were just beginning to dry. No point cleaning the rocks out. I pushed open the window and looked up at the full moon. I put my hands on either side of the frame and pulled myself up on the ledge. I was standing in the window now. Looking down, I saw the Dumpster off to the left. I was directly above the pavement. I was sure I was high enough up ...

Then I heard my name. Below me, Sam screeched the brakes on their bike and stopped. "What are you doing?" They sounded so scared.

"It's okay." I was calm. "Just leave me alone."

"But you're not alone. I'm here!"

Silence.

Then Sam added, "If I leave you alone, you'll leave me alone." They looked around, maybe for help, but there was no one around. "Just step one foot backwards and lower yourself into the room."

"No," I whispered.

Sam's voice became commanding. "It's not for you, you asshole. It's for me. Can you do it for me?"

I pushed open the window and looked up at the full moon. I put my hands on either side of the frame and pulled myself up on the ledge.

I paused. I thought about the overpasses I use to stand on when I was growing up in Calgary. There had been no one there to see me then. No one cared. Now, here, there was someone telling me that I should live. My body hesitantly obeyed.

"Now throw down the keys," Sam instructed.

I found the keys in my pocket and dropped them out the window.

"You have to wait for me to get up there. Okay?"

I paused, and then nodded. It was a promise.

I could hear Sam running up all three flights of stairs as fast as they could with their bike. They opened the front door, threw the bike down in the living room, and rushed into my room.

Sam grabbed my face and looked into my eyes.

I broke. "I fucked everything up!" I wailed.

"No, you didn't. No one's even mad at you," Sam said. "I'm going to get you a glass of water, and then we're both going to go to sleep. Okay?"

"Okay," I burbled through the snot that had run over my mouth.

Sam left the room and reappeared within seconds with two mugs full of tap water. I drank mine and lay down on the side that hurt less. I was shaking like I was soaking wet. Sam lay down behind me and held me. Half-asleep, I tried to get up a couple of times, but Sam held me fast in their arms and said, "It's okay. Go to sleep."

Eventually, the darkness ran out. I opened my eyes and Sam was still holding me. I rolled over towards them and they woke up.

"Stay here," Sam said and went to get more water.

I sat up and we drank in silence.

"I'm glad I got here when I did," Sam said. "You were so drunk last night. I never want to lose you. I'm sorry Riki was at the party. I didn't know they would be there."

"That's okay." My head was pounding. "Sam?"

"Yeah?"

"How am I going to live now?"

Sam knew I had come from a place that had very little love for me. I didn't want to live like that ever again.

"The thing is that you've already started over once," Sam said. "So you can do it again anytime you need to. You know how." Sam looked at me to make sure I understood, and I nodded. "But you can't live here anymore. It's too much. We saw that last night. I'm going to stay with Ocean at their parents' house as long as I can. Is there anywhere you think you could go?"

I mulled it over, coming up blank. Then, "Monster truck rally!" I sang.

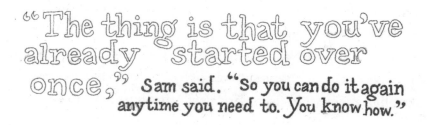

"The thing is that you've already started over once," Sam said. "So you can do it again anytime you need to. You know how."

"What?" Sam looked confused.

"Sorry. I mean Angie. They gave me their number and said I could crash on their couch."

"You want to call them right now?" Sam asked.

I got up and went to the living room, where Emily was looking grumpily at Sam's bike in the middle of the floor.

"I'm sorry, Emily. I had a really bad night and Sam had to come and take care of me."

Emily's eyes softened as they looked at my scabby arm. "No problem. Something to do with Riki, right?"

"Yeah. We broke up. I'm going to move out so you two can live here."

Emily shrugged, and I tried not to take it personally. It's not like they'd ever really expressed an opinion about anything else.

"Can I borrow your phone to call Angie?" I asked.

I took Emily's phone back to my room and dialled the number Angie had given me, but when they picked up, I had trouble speaking. Sam took the phone out of my hand and went into the other room, where I could hear Sam talking but not what they said.

They returned with a big smile on their face. "So, Angie said you can couch surf at their house as long as you want. They live at First and Commercial, so you won't have to go far. You can take your stuff there tomorrow. Here's the address. Now I'm going to find Riki to tell them to stay away until then."

I smiled and squeezed Sam's arm.

"I have to go now," Sam said. "Will you be okay to stay here until tomorrow?"

I nodded. After last night, I knew that Sam loved me. They were a friend that I could hold on to, and I wasn't going to leave them.

"Maybe go back to sleep," Sam suggested and hoisted their bike over their head to go down the stairs.

I lay down and listened to the seagulls outside in the full throes of their day. Maybe they were mourning their cousins, the chickens at the factory. Maybe they were fighting over doughnuts. I drifted off to the sound of their screams.

CHAPTER 19

A beam of midday sunlight moved onto my arm. I felt like I had no skin, but the warmth was nice. I looked over at the window. I had almost lost myself last night, but the sun was out and I could tell it was going to be a bright day.

I got up, went to the kitchen, and filled my mug with more water. Downtown Vancouver shone through the living room window in a way I hadn't seen before. The condo towers looked like crowded teeth in a shark's mouth. Where one stood, two more were waiting to replace it. Would they march down Hastings Street one day until the entire city was made

The condo towers looked like crowded teeth in a shark's mouth.

up of green glass ghosts? All I wanted was to get away from those buildings.

The number 20 bus came quickly, and I was at Broadway and Commercial in minutes. I got on the 99 B-Line heading along Broadway and slipped into a window seat. We passed Granville Street and tears welled in my eyes as I thought of the day I'd arrived here. The image of myself throwing beer on Riki and Lane pushed its way inside my head and shame scaled my throat. I had been angry for good reason. Yet I knew what I'd done was wrong. Someday maybe I would get the chance to apologize, but that wouldn't be anytime soon.

The bus arrived at the university. I got off, walked for a bit, and arrived at the stairs down to Wreck Beach. This time, I counted them as I descended. Riki was right. There were exactly 473 steps. My feet touched sand at the bottom. Now I was as far as I could get from Calgary without swimming. The beach was crowded, but being here alone made it easier to be around hundreds of naked people. Someone at DV8 had told me that students would often see their professors naked at Wreck Beach. That made me smile.

I leaned against a log and closed my eyes. I had always hated the sun in Alberta. It was fluorescent, even through closed eyelids. I imagined it was as close to being in a microwave as a human could survive. Yet this sunlight was golden and warm. The heat radiated through my clothes and soothed the scrapes and bruises from my fall. I focused my ears on the waves rhythmically hitting the shore. Not long ago I had slept here with Riki, but it was the sea that compelled me now. Without a second thought, I took off my shirt. I hadn't felt wind on my torso much in my life. I took off my shorts, socks, and shoes and placed them in a neat pile on top of my shirt. Standing in my underwear, I could see where my body had slid along the asphalt. I scuffed through the sand towards the water as the surf slapped out of time with my steps. The cold was abrupt, making my skin jump, and the salt stung my cuts. When I was submerged up to my neck, I dunked my head under with a sense of completion. So much better than a baptism.

Beauty was all around me now, but I felt apart from it.

Beauty was all around me now, but I felt apart from it. Questions floated up in front of me. For a moment, I ducked, as if a hand were coming from the sky to hit me. Why couldn't I live a day without thinking about dying? Why was I hurting other people? How could I stop hurting myself? Does being hurt turn you into the same kind of person as the one who hurt you? I needed to get away from myself. I wanted to shed my body so I could become someone new. But there was nowhere I could go where I wouldn't still be myself. Maybe if I were more perfect, people would love me, but I felt like I was ten dogs on a leash and, once in a while, I would lose control.

Suddenly, I heard a snap, like a piano string breaking, like a ligament tearing. I erupted, punching and kicking the water. The white-hot rage that I carried poured out like lava into the ocean for I don't know how long. It turned out that the void had no more answers than the recently abandoned Pentecostal god of my childhood. I only stopped thrashing when I felt close to drowning. Heaving for air, I floated up onto my back, the same person, still.

As I walked out of the water, the wind blew warm across my body. I collapsed onto the sand next to my clothes and lay with my arms crossed over my face, waiting for my breath to slow down. The sun was already drying the beads of water all over my body. I saw myself standing on the window ledge again. I almost hadn't made it to this day, but my body kept breathing without me asking it to. I just had to keep going.

EPILOGUE

I pushed open the back door of the Brickhouse and rushed outside. The street lights glinted yellow off every surface in the alley as I wobbled to squat and take a piss. There had been a long lineup for the washrooms in the bar, and I couldn't wait. The lights above were big and blurry. The warmth flowed out of me and I smelled it pooling around my shoes.

A moment later, people started appearing like zombies in a movie. First a few, and then a horde. I was invisible until one of them spotted me, cocked their head, and shouted, "Hey, are you taking a shit?"

Then someone in the middle of the crowd yelled, "No, they're pissing!"

I couldn't escape. If I jumped up, I'd flash everyone. Instead, I chose to stay squatting and let each inquisitive face give me a once-over, while I silently hoped none of them took it as an invitation to fuck with me.

That's when I spotted my new roommate, Ben. We'd come here to have some getting-to-know-you drinks, and I had gotten to know a few too many.

"Hey," they said casually, like I was standing up with my pants still on. "I'm going to wait at the end of the alley. Catch up in a minute?"

"Sure."

The bartender poked their head out the back door as I was standing up. "Really nice," they said. "Come on, we have toilets inside. As if this alley doesn't smell bad enough."

I grunted an apology and walked down the alley to meet Ben. They were standing with their fingers laced through the fence around the Jimi Hendrix shrine.

"So cool Jimi used to live here with their grandma," Ben said.

"Yeah," I said, still shaking with shame. "So cool."

The shame came for me the hardest in the morning, as it had every day since I'd moved to Vancouver a year ago. I crawled up the stairs to my music manager's apartment from my basement suite. We lived in Strathcona, on different floors of a house on Princess Avenue. Hana had introduced us. I think they dated a little bit after Hana and I broke up. I never asked because it didn't feel much like my business. I had started over again a few times since then.

The shame came for me the hardest in the morning, as it had every day since I'd moved to Vancouver a year ago.

I was releasing an album and I was going to play lots of shows all over Vancouver that summer. I was living my actual dream.

My manager was fifteen years older than me, and I knew they'd been sober for at least ten years. They cracked open their front door when I knocked and said, "Hey, kid. Come in."

I liked how they called me that. I didn't have many older people in my everyday life anymore. I sat down on the loveseat in their kitchen while they made coffee for us with an Italian stovetop pot. It hissed loudly as I tried to form a reason for my visit.

"What's up?" they eventually asked.

"I don't know," I said. "I guess I'm tired of acting in ways that I can't control ..."

"What happened?" they asked.

"I was way drunker than I meant to get last night."

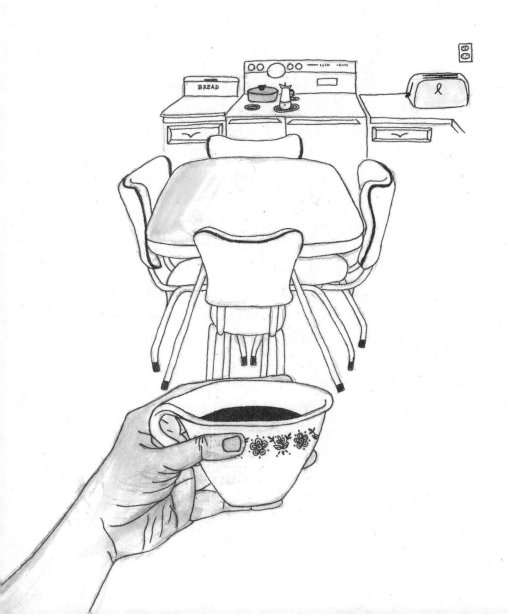

"Was anyone with you? You're not drinking alone again, are you?" My manager had had to come pick me up from the Astoria a few times in their truck when I'd gotten confused about who I was and how to get home. We never talked about it the next day, but I knew they worried about me. So I'd promised to bring a buddy when I was out drinking.

"No, but that made it worse. I was totally humiliated in front of my new roommate." I looked at them, hungry for a solution.

"You know that there's one thing all of your hard situations have in common, right?" They waited.

"Yeah. They always happen when I've been drinking."

"I used to have lots of problems. Not the same as yours, but I was very out of control. I was into alcohol and tons of drugs. I was living the life with my hardcore band. Most of the time it was awesome, but once in a while I would end up in the biggest shitstorms and I didn't know how I got there."

I nodded knowingly.

"One day, I woke up and realized that my actions contributed to the chaos that I lived in. I did the math. It was always me plus booze and drugs. So, that morning, about fifteen years ago, I quit. Have you tried quitting before?" they asked.

I shook my head. There was a pause, and then I earnestly inquired, "How?"

"Well, you just stop."

It was a brief answer, but it didn't feel curt or impatient. I puzzled over it. My manager put a mug down in front of me.

"I think I understand," I said as I blew the steam off the top of my coffee.

It was a new day, and I just had to start over again, one more time.

Notes from the Author and the Illustrator

RAE SPOON

In *Green Glass Ghosts*, as with many of my fiction works, the main character is placed by age, location, and other factors quite close to my own experience. I moved to Vancouver in 2000, and although this book is fictionalized, I included the trajectory, the many struggles, and the high points I experienced when I finally got to start over in a new place. I wanted to show how lacking traditional family structures forces people to look for those bonds elsewhere with mixed results. I also wanted to encapsulate how lost I felt being thrown into the world with a lifelong skill set that didn't match what I was going to have to figure out.

I grew up in a strict yet ethically skewed Pentecostal home on Treaty 7 territory in Calgary. In becoming an adult, being queer and trans is only one of the many chasms that I've crossed that makes the world I grew up in one I can't abide. The complex post-traumatic stress disorder I deal with on a daily basis is a result of the heavy trauma I experienced as a young child. I know I've failed many times, but my goal is to not hurt other people the same way that I was hurt. I would do anything to break that cycle of abuse. Sometimes it feels like I have generations weighing on my shoulders. I'm trying to change the cycles of intergenerational trauma and abuse, and it's heavy work.

I used to think my trauma made me worth less than other people. Now I'm working on seeing my trauma as neutral. For a long time, I would try to not talk about it, but this led to explosions. The people I met when I first arrived in Vancouver saw the most unstable side of me. Getting help for mental health was very stigmatized then, and some people close to me judged my attempts to get medication or counselling. As a queer and trans person, it was very hard for me to find a good counsellor. Many of my attempts at finding a therapist were harmful to me.

When I was drinking or on other substances, the cracks in my ability to maintain a linear timeline would show, and I would end up with dangerous people in places I didn't recognize. Several incidents were severe enough that I came to understand that if I didn't quit drinking, I would die. It took me two tries (once when I was twenty-one for three years, and finally when I was twenty-five, which has lasted for fourteen years). The longer stretch I'm on now has been sustained with counselling and medication when I've needed them. I need support and stability to live my life embodied and feeling all the things that still come up as difficult.

Gem Hall and I have been friends for many years, and I've always been captivated by their art. We figured out early on that there are many parallels between our experiences. The commonality of moving to Vancouver as new adults with very little family support is one of them. Working with Gem was central to my desire to create this book, and I'm so pleased to have their voice be part of it.

GEM HALL

Green Glass Ghosts is a project that is very dear to my heart. Living transiently in many cities across so-called Canada/ Turtle Island; facing lifelong issues with securing housing and conforming to colonial societal expectations as an itinerant person; struggling with mental health and addiction issues from a young age; surviving abuse and also being a current resident of so-called Vancouver's Downtown Eastside, I find Rae's story to be deeply familiar on many levels. As much as this is Rae's story, this collaboration has also allowed me to tell parts of my own parallel story in a visual language.

I wanted this book to feel like you were right there in the illustrations, which is why I used the angles and perspective I did. I chose watercolour to evoke the feeling of the Coast Salish land and the ocean and the rain cycles, and to depict the characters as spirits in most of the images, with a couple of exceptions. I wanted to play off the title, to acknowledge the way the city often feels dense with spirits to me, as well as to reflect the way you can feel a bit like a ghost of a person when floating around in a new city or moving from place to place. Yet there are also those moments when you feel more human in those experiences, like when Rae and Riki are walking in East Van looking for jobs for Rae, or when Rae decides to quit drinking.

By painting in colour while also knowing that most images would be printed in black and white, like a photocopy, I was also paying tribute to a DIY zine aesthetic. I specifically avoided using a ruler or perfecting the perspective of each image; I wanted to give a feeling of distortion and intoxication. This also reflects the way I learned to illustrate, when I was homeless and drawing in transit. Before now, my work has only ever been self-published or appeared in anthologies self-published by others. I deeply value these forms of print media, and I encourage anyone who is unfamiliar with zines and self-published works (especially any aspiring writers and artists!) to look into them. But as much as my illustration style is rooted in zine culture, it's also a great honour to be invited to publish with a press that I respect enormously. I would like to thank Arsenal Pulp Press for amplifying the voices of so many talented writers and artists who otherwise may not have the opportunity to access such a platform.

So many young queer and trans people, and those who struggle with addictions, relocate to the West Coast with dreams of living a better life. Many of us are able to do that, and many of us are not. Surviving many of my contemporaries has been a double-edged sword, and this is an experience Rae and I have gone through together. There's a certain weight to being one of the ones who made it out alive. I believe that healing and recovery are non-linear, and that sobriety is just one approach, while also acknowledging that substance use was a coping mechanism that kept me alive for a long time and helped me connect with others like me. I hope to honour all the lives that have touched mine, especially of those who are not as privileged as I am.

For me, choosing sobriety is an act of choosing to live, and I appreciate the opportunity to help bring Rae's story to life visually since we both share this approach. My hope is that this book will reach other young queer and trans people facing similar struggles and become a lighthouse for others to share their own stories and survival strategies.

Acknowledgments

RAE SPOON

I was born on, live, work, and write on stolen land. Land back now. Solidarity with water protectors and the people whose land this is. Defund the police. Defund the RCMP. This book was written on the traditional and current territory of the Songhees, Esquimalt, and W̱SÁNEĆ peoples.

My editor is the most important part of my writing process. Thanks to Shirarose Wilensky for seeing the strength of the project and refining it to what it is now.

For a large part of the editing process I was in treatment for cancer. Thank you to Kaleb Robertson and Gan for showing me what twenty years of trying to build a family looks like by being the ones I needed to make it through. I hope to spend the next twenty years showing you that you have family in me.

Thank you to Lauren Goldman and Karina Zeidler for going out of your way to support me in an extremely transphobic and/or trans-unaware medical system. I truly believe you're both saving lives every day. You saved mine.

Thanks to Diane Mondor for stepping in at the eleventh hour and being a constant support during my treatment for me and my caregivers. The trajectory of my life would have been far different without you.

Thank you to Island Mountain Arts, Julie Fowler, and Sharon Brown for the time I spent working on this book in Wells, BC, on the shared territory of eight nations: Lhtako, Nazko, Lhoosk'uz, Ulkatcho, ʔEsdilagh, Xatśūll, Simpcw, and Lheidli T'enneh.

GEM HALL

I would like to acknowledge all those who helped support me during the making of this book.

To all the lands I have moved across—the spirits, ancestors, plants, creatures, and bodies of water that I live in relationship with—thank you. It's impossible to give appropriate context for a story set in so-called Vancouver without acknowledging that the Musqueam, Tsleil-Waututh, and Squamish nations are the original peoples and caretakers of this land. Indigenous peoples are over-represented in the street-involved populations in this city, which I understand is a result of the ongoing displacement and genocide of Indigenous peoples and the colonial project that is called Canada. I know that one of the reasons why I survived and have been given the opportunities in life I've been given is my privilege as a settler on these lands, and I think about that every day.

Thank you to Rae Spoon for having my back, believing in me, and entrusting me with your story; to Brian Lam, Jazmin Welch, Shirarose Wilensky, and everyone at Arsenal Pulp Press for all your hours of hard work and dedication; to Sasha Kubicek and Robin Tunnicliffe for all your kind encouragement and nourishment over the years; to Jaime Burnet, Tara-Michelle Ziniuk, Imogen Di Sapia, Kama La Mackerel, Leah Lakshmi Piepzna-Samarasinha, and Cristy Road Carrera for your kind words and praise of this book; to Tara-Michelle Ziniuk for being there and showing me how to survive; to Leah Lakshmi Piepzna-Samarasinha for encouraging my work and looking out for me since I was sixteen; to Jes Dolan for existing and instantly feeling something like home; to Imogen Di Sapia and all my Romani cousins for following the strings of red thread and beads to find me; to Annanda DeSilva for being so safe and good to me for so many years; to Laura Shepherd for being a lighthouse through many storms; to Chandra Melting Tallow for holding on and creating worlds that make it easier for me to exist just by being; to my partner, Gino Daniellè Armandina Andolfatto Mommi (Sorrel), for being exactly who you are—living life alongside you challenges me to dream bigger and become a better version of myself; to Claire Beauvoir, Kiala Löytömäki, Alexa Black, Khalela Leilani, Moe LaVerdure, Arlo Doyle, and the lands and plants that hold us—thank you for creating space that allows me to begin to expand into the fullness of my creative, spiritual, and ancestral potential; to Dr Sutherland, Dr Lysak, and Shannon Raison for treating me like a human being and helping me rebuild my livelihood; to all my Almas for your shelter and care; to Daisy Shea and Faye Bontje for building a future that could include me and for supporting me in queer community as a survivor; to Drew W for all your support and for being a living example that a good sober future is possible; to Emmis Ayda for saving my life; and to all those we have lost, with special thanks to Iseult O'Flynn-Magee, Vic Horvath, and Rosalee Davis—may you rest in peace.

My art and survival rest on the backs of all those who have gone before me.